THE EPIC DIALOGS OF MHYO

AN ADULT FAIRY TALE

by

CHARLES NUETZEL

The Borgo Press
An Imprint of Wildside Press

MMVII

FIRST EDITION

CONTENTS

INTRODUCTION

This book is being presented as an "adult" fairy tale. But it is far more than that. What follows is based on the only existing record of a very ancient document, *The Dialogs of Mhyo*. The original text was discovered several decades ago in a small shop in India. Since then it has been in the possession of Col. Joseph C. Gaberial. When he died, his nephew, J. Clifford Davis, found it among many other items in the man's private collection of artifacts. It was obviously very old, on parchment paper and tied together with a small red ribbon. Mr. Davis gave it to the local museum. The director, Dr. Thomas Gordon Waymans III, was able to translate it into English. J. Clifford Davis acquired a photocopy of the original text and a copy of the translation, both of which his son Carlton Davis showed the present publisher's wife.

Even a casual reading reveals that, while very ancient, the text was collected from much older source material, quite obviously lost in time. This is, in fact, a collected "anthology" of incomplete quotes and scenes.

There is much evidence that the original "myth," upon which this document seems to have been based, was nothing but a fairy tale. Though some experts in ancient text have their doubts concerning the whole project, there are enough who believe that all myths are based, at least in part, on actual historical events. There are many people, the most prominent being Dr. Major James C. Clarment, III, who believe the original text to relate to a very real warrior general of an ancient land, perhaps still undiscovered. Perhaps these "Epic Dialogs" are the only evidence of its existence. Perhaps, perhaps, perhaps. Nobody knows, for certain, its exact origins.

For this edition a few editorial liberties have been taken in order to offer something that can reach the widest possible audience. (The original text can be found elsewhere in libraries devoted to preserving such specialized material.)

The publisher believes that The Dialogs, in the present form, will not only find a place on the shelves of today's reader, but in the libraries of those who follow us in the 21st Century and beyond.

[Editorial Note: Throughout the body of the "Dialogs" brackets are used in this manner to indicate missing material: [...]. At places where we are uncertain concerning some word or words they will be enclosed is brackets in the same manner.]

—Charles Nuetzel
Thousand Oaks, California
July 2006

Once up on a Timer

Once up on a Time there was a land that we will simply call the World of Walls.

[...]

As in all good fairy tales there is, in this world of Walls that spoke, this, we might call it, mythical land—universe—many legends, fantasies, witches, and wizards. Most importantly there is Godwall and Deathwall. Of course, these Walls that speak created conflicts between the People of the lands. [...] Warriors were sent forth to slay dragons and do great battle against evil wizards. In such a manner heroes won the hearts of noble women by bold and daring deeds.

I believe that just about tells the beloved Myth as we have all learned to accept it.

[...]

But we must always remember that in the lands of Godwall and Deathwall all may be nothing more than illusional reality.

[Editor's note: This "Once up on a Time" is from the *Dialogs of Mhyo*, and it reveals the Events of Mhyo's First Conflict against Deathwall.]

His Audience with Godwall

"So you wish to become more than you are?" Godwall spoke for the first time, voice seeming to bounce off the shocking white walls of Its Holy Temple. "And whom is it that would say you are worthy of becoming more than you are?"

Silence answered It. Because the large, powerfully built young man standing there in front of the awesome Deity found it difficult to even think of anything to say, let alone make use of his voice. All his life he had waited for this moment when Godwall would give him Audience as was prescribed by Law. He had rehearsed a speech of many profound and simple statements all of which merely announced he was ready for his assigned post in life. Now he stood before the Beloved Ruler, the Creative Deity that directed the True destiny of all the People, and was unable to speak. He felt no fear of being struck down instantly by some deadly ray or killing beam. That was not Godwall's way. Yet the anxiety, the uncertainly, the very fact of this experience was overwhelming.

"Answer me, you are human, you have a body, you have a head, you have a brain, you have a tongue, you have a mouth, let them speak, form words and answer my question. Who is it that would

8

say you are worthy of becoming more than you are?"

"I do not wish to become more than I am, only to learn what I am to be."

"The same thing. All the same thing."

"But—"

"Who is this that stammers before me? Speak!"

"Mhyo...Janton," he managed.

"I know that. But who is Mhyo Janton?"

If Godwall did not know the answer then what or who would know? Godwall certainly knew all there was to know about the People. Many Learned Ones of great Nobility and Status suggested that It even knew more about Deathwall than was generally suspected or reported in the Folk Papers.

"Who is a Mhyo Janton?" Godwall demanded, not really having waited for an answer to the first question. "Where is there a man, for that matter, who could answer a question concerning his identity without knowing all there is to know? No where. There is no such man. Nobody knows all things. Except, perhaps, myself! But I am Godwall. So, that's a different matter. Thus it must be a nobody who is given the mission of self discovery. For if one is somebody, they know what they are—which is very little if they are totally honest with themselves. A nobody much admit knowing nothing— and thus be willing to discover knowledge of the world around them. Only thus can they decide if they are more than nothing. But then he might discover he is nobody—or that simply there is no difference between a nobody and a somebody other than understanding the fine difference...understand?"

9

Mhyo Janton, of course, did not understand a word that Godwall spoke. It, like all gods and wizards and witches went out of Its way to be confusing; or so it would seem. That was, naturally, the way of all gods.

"You do understand the importance of being a nobody?"

Godwall quite obviously required, demanded, commanded, decreed an answer. The very tone of his voice left no doubt about the matter.

"I...yes..." Mhyo Janton lied.

"Yes. No. Maybe. And then...well, sometimes. Women's words. Maybe I love you, of course, means: yes I do love you; only you must win me through daring deeds. Or she might say, no, I do not love you and I can never love you. All of which means the same: Go and prove yourself worthy of my love. Maybe then I'll admit that I do love you. All words that have little true meaning. Confusion. Illusion. Masks. Scripts. Mere walls to restrict, mystify, confound. But so it is with the People. Beyond the walling mask is another and beyond one convoluted script a more complicated one. One wonders where the real mask or scripts hide. Surely under the final real mask must be the utterly foolish and stupid and useless self that one never wants to reveal to the world—or to himself. Well, herself, too, if you want to be fair concerning the total confusion that is female. It is all the same to me. I really cannot see the difference between man and woman; oh, a few little physical differences, I'll admit, but not enough to make an issue of. Well, never mind. The fact is you do no know what I mean because you are a nobody. Being a nobody you deserve to begin your adult experience by learning what you are: somebody or no-body or maybe a no thing

"As it is written, as it is so computed in the history of events, you are the son of Miij Hanna and Tol Janton. Your parents were very common farmers, who have toiled hard to survive. They have made it possible for you to enter the School of Heroes in order for you to become a Warrior. You have been a good son. You worked hard in the fields of your father's small food-growing farm. You have honed your warrior's skills and have built yourself a strong body. You exist, you breathe, you have suffered childhood and you have enjoyed the friendship of a man called Golter, who has become your servant by choice of my words. This just about covers it. And now you stand before me and wish to become even more than you are in order to win Princess Ginnia."

Godwall became suddenly silent, as if out of breath, though, of course, it did not breathe.

Mhyo Janton stood there waiting nervously. He had worn a finely woven Warrior's garment of silken white cloth. It draped tightly about his wonderfully handsome, muscular form, belted at the waist by a thick, white strap of the finest leather. A simple warrior's sword hung from the belt.

It was soon obvious that Godwall would say no more. When the prolonged silence became too painful, Mhyo Janton said: "I have come to learn, I have come to embrace Godwall's blessing and be assigned to my unit and—"

"Rot! You have come to seek wisdom and to seek understanding and to learn about yourself and to know what the future might bring. And you have come before Godwall to discover what it is you must do in life. You wish to know what you must do to gain honor in our lands. What, must you do in the name of Godwall to become accepted as a fine and true Warrior? Now is that not right? But, of course it is. And that is one hell of a lot, if you ask me. In fact, a bit too much!"

Silence followed, like black, liquid ice. Desperately, Mhyo Janton offered: "I come to understand."

"What? What the future holds? I will tell you what to understand—is that it?—and everything will be simple, and you will not find it necessary to think too much or to move aimlessly through life without a goal. Is that not correct?"

"I come to offer my service. To you. Godwall." Mhyo desperately countered.

"What kind of service could you offer that I would consider of any value? What could a simple nobody, a no thing, offer a God?"

"Willingness to serve?"

"That is quite obvious by the very fact that you are standing there before me. Okay. You wish direction. You wish to serve. You wish to please. You wish to do that which will make it possible for you to discover why you are a nobody. You wish to correct that condition and become a titled somebody. Okay. Then I offer you simply this:

"Seek your answer from Deathwall!

"Only from the Voice of Deathwall will you learn what you wish to know. But remember: It is not always the end results that offers the greatest rewards. It is through the process of discovery that we learn the most. It is the movement from beginning to end that reveals the real truth.

12

"Go to Deathwall. Ask Deathwall: 'How can I become more than I am?'

"And, my bold nobody friend, Deathwall will be more than eager to offer many wondrous and marvelous answers. It will tell you how to begin your search of discovery. Deathwall is a Wall of many voices and a very powerful and destructive Voice it is.

"Through Deathwall's wisdom one could quickly learn the way to become more than they are. But you must penetrate beyond the very barrier of Its existence to truly understand anything.

"Of course nobody has successfully managed that; but warriors who survive the mission and return to me, have, at least, learned how very difficult it is to become more than they are.

"If you survive and return you will truly have earned a place of some value here in my domain. Go. And don't return until you have become more than you are."

Godwall was silent. It was a long silence. It continued and would not end. Then the bright glare of the room dimmed, as if the deity had gone to sleep.

Mhyo Janton slowly realized the interview had ended. He had experienced the first, and perhaps only, meeting with Godwall. Having been given his assigned duty he slowly turned and left the magnificent Temple of Godwall to begin his journey.

A FRIEND AND SERVANT, GOLTER

"What did Godwall say?" the beefy, muscular young Golter quickly asked, as Mhyo Janton stepped up to him. The man and two horses stood just outside the magnificent temple. The clean lines of the building lifted up around Godwall, encasing It in a shimmering pure white cylinder that disappeared into the billowy clouds above.

"What did It say," Golter repeated.

"To seek...Deathwall."

Golter shuttered, visibly, as if attempting to shake off vile insects creeping into his arm pits. His large lips drooped for but a moment, then slowly spoke, as if finding the words difficult to form. "Deathwall? But...why? Has he doomed you to die? Even before beginning your magnificent career as a Wonderful Warrior of the Folks? Does it all end now?"

Mhyo Janton glanced at the huge Temple, considered the tip that penetrated the distant clouds. The Wall to which this large cylinder was attached, continued in both directions, to the very horizons. This Wall was a never-ending barrier between the World of the Folk and the Mysterious Void that surely must lay beyond.

What might be beyond the Wall, Mhyo wondered. What was the Wall really hiding? Was there

14

anything at all beyond it? What could possibly exist behind this Wall of the Gods? Perhaps the Universal answers to Universal Questions! Nobody really knew, for no living person, creature, monster or Wizard had ever left the Land of the Walls.

Actually, Mhyo wondered why anyone would want to leave the protective heaven of this Eden. The Lands had just about everything one would want. Not only were there the Working Folk, but the Gods, and all the Wizards and Warriors and Dragons and Magical forces and Powers and so many exciting, places to explore. Or, at least, so he'd been told. Of course, Mhyo had never been more than half a day's ride from his parent's farm.

Now things would change.

He could be busy for the rest of his life, even if he lived forever more, just exploring the Land of the Walls. Why would anybody want to go Beyond the Walls?

A strange and disturbing concept, he realized..

Thus his thoughts continued to torment him for some time. Such thoughts circled back and forth, coiled around each other until choking all reasonable conclusions.

When the silence stretched beyond a reasonable period, Golter broke it: "But Deathwall has deadly rays and beams and the Power of Death. Why, in Godwall's name, would one want to face It? And..."

"I know." Mhyo Janton shrugged, helplessly, resigned to his assigned duty. What could he do other than what Godwall demanded? Everybody must do what the Deity demanded. It was expected. And the People always did what was expected of them. After all, the farmers farmed, didn't they? Warriors warred! And pretty little Princess' tormented and teased their doting warriors...

Golter's voice faded back into focus, chewing away at Mhyo's thoughts. "...but that is not an Assignment, it is not a Rank in any Army, it is not a Commission. I thought that's why you were appearing before Godwall."

"I know." Maybe felt a bit tired, disappointed. "I know. But Godwall's ways are mysterious and we must follow his commands, as we willingly follow his Laws."

"Was that...all Godwall said? Go before Deathwall?"

"There was a lot more. But I have to think as I ride...come, let's get away from here." The young Warrior glanced once again at the Temple of Godwall, repressing a shiver. His eyes followed those clean, gleaming walls, that stretched off into the distance, disappearing into those bright fleecy clouds.

Without another word the two men mounted the horses and started down the neatly gardened pathway. Off in the distance the road lead to rolling hills spotted by lovely deep green trees.

It was a beautifully warm, sunny day, but Mhyo Janton felt none of the excitement and thrill he had experienced before entering the Temple of Godwall. Now he experienced an empty disappointment, a slight edge of uncertain, nagging anxiety.

It was a long time before he spoke.

"Do you understand how being a somebody can make you a nobody and that being a nobody is...I guess, better than being a somebody?

The other man's laughter exploded on the lands. "What does that mean? Foolishness. Insanity. The ideas of a madman. Only a Fool would talk that way. Only—"

"Godwall. Godwall spoke those words!"

Golter gasped. His huge head jerked, turned, glanced at the distant temple they had left behind them. He looked as if he expected lightening to strike them blind. "God...wall?"

"Yes, Godwall."

"Want does it mean? Then..." Golter sounded desperate.

"I don't know."

Golter muttered, under his breath: "Somebody. Nobody. Foolishness? Forgive me...Godwall...but I'm only a simple person, a mere servant and I don't understand such..." His voice got louder and higher pitched as he continued: "But I am convinced there surely must be great and wonderful and powerful meaning to anything Godwall might say. Even if I, a dumb fool servant—and humble, I might add—who does not understand." The man glance behind them as if hoping Godwall would understand—and Forgive—him. "I am nothing, if but a servant fool..." The words faded, as the men continued riding along the dirt road.

After a long while, Golter, apparently beyond his earlier confusion and fear, asked, in an almost conversational manner: "Where are we going? I mean, right now?"

"Directly at right angles to Godwall. If you must know the exact facts as I understand them to be. That is the Direction, so I've been told, to find the path that leads to Deathwall. You should know that. Everybody knows that. We all know that from birth. That's our Birthright."

"No. No. No. I meant...now. Right now. Where are we going. Today. This moment. Now. Out to kill a dragon?" He sounded almost hopeful, as if such an adventure would certainly delay the journey to Deathwall. "Though, quite frankly, I'm not overly anxious to come face to face with a dangerous, meat-eating, monster TerribleRex Dragon. At least, not right now, here at the very beginning of our Grand Adventure Together. I just fear them less than I do Deathwall. Dragons can be a drag, so I'm told. So...well...I'm simply in no rush to thrill to their overwhelming killer jaws and crushing, scraping claws. Even with you, Mighty Warrior, Dragon-Killer-to-be at my side. In no hurry at all. You can believe me. You sure can. No hurry to run into no dangerous Drags."

Mhyo Janton laughed heartily at that. "I've been up against enough dragons for one morning." A gleam of desire flared in his eyes. "I thought maybe we could arrange to see—"

Golter's arms few up in the air, as he cried out in mock-horror: "Don't say it. Don't. Please!" He knew his friend well enough to understand that gleam of desire. "Don't say it. I don't want to hear ONE word "

"But—"

"Anything but that! Deathwall would be safer than...her. Please, don't force me, master, to be a party to this terrible deed. Give me Drags. Anything. Even Deathwall!" His words were filled with quite convincing terror. "You know how Princess Ginnia's father feels."

"I know." The magnificent warrior sounded dejected, though a wide grin spread across his handsome lips. "Anyway...he's not home right now. Ginnia is alone."

"That's bad enough. Bad enough. Do you have any idea what might...happen?"

"Tell me."

"Anything. The female is a very mysterious and dangerous creature. Well, for men like you. That is. You are very...well, idealistic when it comes to maidens. And she is—well...she is—

"Wonderful."

"So you say. All men think their women are wonderful. Tell me something new."

"She's the woman I love."

"So. I said tell me something new."

"She's the princess I will win by great deeds."

"That is if you survive Deathwall."

Ignoring that, the young warrior said: "She's a—"

"A spoiled brat." Golter stated in a matter-of-fact manner.

"Of course. All Princess are spoiled. It is their very nature. Otherwise they would hardly be called a Princess. The title defines."

Golter merely nodded, then, after a moment, stated in an almost all-too reasonable voice: "Then her father, quite naturally, is no different from all fathers. And he believes that no man is good enough for his daughter. Until such a man proves himself—or whatever. Fathers are fathers because they Father." The last was almost a direct quote from the Dictionary of the Folk. Then added: "Not just sperm donors, either."

"Really. You can be so crude."

"Crude? I'm just your basic, common servant."

"Does that mean you have to be crude?

"Your problem is you're too shy with the maiden sex. Now, as for me, since I'm just a common folk servant, maidens are to be made...love to."

"I agree. And I love her."

"I talking about being loved...in a ravishing way. Mount them like you would your...mount. Attack them like you would the enemy. Conquer them. Body, mind and soul."

"Mind, soul, then body."

"Whatever."

"You have it backwards, Golter. Mind, soul, then body."

"Wizard lizards! You have it backwards. Gaze upon the treasures before offering your life—"

"Look, but don't touch."

"Seeing isn't believing. Experiencing the touch, the feel, the texture, the very innards of your woman is what life is all about."

"You are crude." Though the expression in the Warrior's eyes was quite envious. There was no doubt that Mhyo held a great passion for his Princess. "You're crude to the point of being—"

"I'm blunt, unlearned in the finer arts. But I know the fine joys of wanton pleasures. I know what a maiden is there for. I know—"

"Too much for a young servant."

"I know what to do with a maiden."

"I know to protect all maidens, Warrior-fashion."

"Sure, I know that. You bought into the con that maidens are ladies and pure and innocent and should be respected and protected and—"

"Warriors are Gentleman." Mhyo sounded proud as he continued: "And to be a Gentleman—"

"Does not mean being a fool," Golter finished for him.

"I thought we were talking about Princess—"

"Yes, yes. But her father. Remember? What about her father. Remember that father's father."

"I know. Name defines. And daughters daughter."

Golter's eyes made a dramatic skyward movement of repressed mock-confusion. "Whatever that means."

"Means a lot to them." The young warrior's mouth tightened, stubbornly.

"I suppose. But, anyway, I think you are a wonderful and fine fellow, a future grand and mighty Warrior. But the Princess and her Father—"

"Just want me to prove myself."

"Just as the Father/Daughter Book demands," came the almost shuttering retort.

Mhyo shrugged. "Fine with me. Quite honestly it almost makes more sense than what Godwall said."

Golter chose to make no comment about Godwall. He had experienced his moment with it; that was only two days ago. His Audience had been very short, and far more satisfying, at the time. Godwall had simply said: "Be Mhyo Janton's servant; that is enough for you to be."

"Why must we see Princess Ginnia?" he asked, with just the edge of mockery to his voice. As if he didn't know!

"To say good-bye, of course."

"I...well, guess I should do my...well...good-byes to Mara..." There was a wicked gleam in his eyes.

"You treat her like a gutter-slut."

"I simply treat her like a passionate, wonderful, full-bodied woman should be treated."

"Must you—"

"I must! And if you had any...well...er...well... guts..."

"Don't hesitate! Say it. Hurt me. Damn me. Stick it to me! BALLS. Right? You wanted to say Balls."

"Well, if you had them you'd use them!"

"There's a time and a place. By the Rules—"

"By the Rules my foot. I might not war like you; I might even be considered, by many, a shivering, cowardly fool. But I know what a maiden is there for. A maiden is to be...made — love to."

"I think we covered...er... uncovered...that topic."

"Well, you do it your way—I'll be a crude servant and have my pleasures with my chosen maiden. And I will not settle for anything so small as a silly little kiss." The twinkle in his beady eyes communicated lustfully blunt desire.

Mhyo Janton laughed. "Considering our conversation I do believe you'd take advantage of this young woman..."

"Hardly, I'll let her take advantage of me. Women do the seduction; not the men. I may be a fool, or even as crude as you say, but when it comes to the maiden class—"

"You take advantage of them."

22

"Advantage? No such thing. I just give 'em what they want de mostest! A maiden wants pretty much the same thing a man wants...when it comes to matters of...love."

"Maybe maidens are different from Princess—"

"We live only once—and I will gladly embrace all Mara wishes to offer. In fact, I'll embrace all de maidens that offer themselves up as delicious deserts to travel-tired Warriors and their servants." Grinning eagerly, he added: "I'll take 'em all on! And ask for more!"

"And I will do what is right and proper, as any and all good Warriors have been taught to do, and honor my princess' highest desires. Law dictates she must have the standards of a Princess, otherwise, by definition, she wouldn't be—"

"And if a princess' were to offer a kiss...or more?"

Mhyo Janton felt a hot surge of desire flush up through him. The idea of embracing the Princess was enough to inspire him to attempt the most impossible deeds Godwall might demand. He would kill the greatest Dragon in the Land of Speaking Walls if it would win him a passionate kiss from this princess he loved so much.

But, of course, a true and Royal Princess would never submit to such desires without the Wedding Ring. There were Rules; and the People of the Lands surely must follow all the Rules, otherwise the Walls might come tumbling down.

What a horrible thought!

"Enough!" Mhyo cried, spurring his horse into a rapid run. "Enough to say good-bye to my Princess!"

"Enough," his companion roared in quick pursuit, "to do good-bye to my maiden."

Enough, thought Mhyo, longingly, to but touch the lips of a Princess. He didn't dare to let himself continue that wicked and overwhelming thought. Instead he let himself experience the chilling wind on his face as the horse raced up the hill towards the castle of his beloved Princess.

IN THE GARDEN OF THE PRINCESS

When Mhyo Janton told Princess Ginnia what had happened at his audience with Godwall, she drew back a delicate head in deep thought. She looked very lovely in her puzzled anger. "How can you claim to love me when you don't even know who you are?"

"That's not what I said!"

"Then what is it you did say?"

"Well...well..."

"Well...did not Godwall tell you to go out and discover what you are?"

"How to become more than I am."

"Same thing." she stubbornly observed, standing there very primly, the flowing blue filmy lace of her gown folding beautifully about that delicate princess frame.

"Well...I guess," he replied, uncertain, but not willing to argue the point. "Makes no sense to me—"

"Well I'm certain Godwall understands!" she snapped, angrily. "Godwall understands all there is to know in the Lands. It wouldn't suggest that you do something that did not make sense. Now would It?"

Mhyo signed. "What's the use?"

"Well, if you don't know...well, honestly, Mhyo!" She stamped her foot like all good princesses were supposed to do when miffed. "You say you love me. And you object to doing what Godwall says you must do in order to gain status and thus win the hand of the woman you so boldly claim—with your mouth—to love. If you aren't willing to do as Godwall tells you, how can I believe you truly love me? Tell me that?"

"I'm not saying—"

Shaking her head in anger, she blurted: "Oh, father is right!"

"Why?"

"A Warrior is not worth much until he has gone out to slay his required number of Dragons—and thus prove himself worthy of a true and fine princess' love—and let you become the father of her children, the master of her life, the man with whom she is willing to follow—"

"Well, what do you want?" Women could be impossible; especially a pretty young Princess.

"Oh, Mhyo. Can't you see? Godwall is right. One has to learn how they can become more than...or whatever...they are...before they can ever consider taking on the responsibilities of a woman's love. And think of the family, the children!"

She hesitated, lovely forehead crinkling in very deep thought. She looked beautiful as she frowned in that manner. But then, Mhyo was a sucker for this one and only Princess.

"He did say you had to go to..." She paused, as if the next word was so horrible that it was near impossible to say. "Deathwall...to learn about—"

"Well, yes." He puffed up, proud at the apparent fear that dreaded Deity of the Lands created in this young princess.

"Then good!" she stated, reasonably enough. "Then you must go."

She was learning so very close to him that it was difficult to ignore custom. He wanted to draw her form against his own and kiss that lovely full mouth. Those lips were now half parted into blatant, hungry passion. Regardless of his conversation with Golter, only a short time ago, he had passions, desires, dreams, fantasies—totally crude and unseemly; not those of a Gentlemen Warrior. He had to admit, silently, privately, to himself that he wanted far more than mere looking at the treasures that might someday become his rewards for daring deeds. It would be vulgar, disgusting, delightful, horrible, wonderful, terrible, fantastic to take wanton liberties with this magnificent, pure, innocent, perfect Princess of his Heart. What would this proud, virginal young princess think of such boldness, such raw, brutal, passionate animal desire? Most of all what would she think of his Sense of Honor?

And what would her father think?

This last stopped him cold.

A light touch of pride flirted in her blue eyes as they gazed up anxiously into his. "Well? Isn't there something...you would like..." The Princess' voice, trembling slightly, failed, the words breathed out to nothingness. Finally she took a deep breath, stiffened, then snapped: "Well?"

"Well?" he muttered, half turning, now afraid that his manly control would shatter. It was almost overwhelming, this haunting spell she was now creating by her very presence. It was, really, too much. Even for a powerful young warrior like himself. In fact: especially for such a magnificent young male animal. After all he was a Warrior in his prime!

"Oh! Well!" she cursed; most un-princess-like. "Well go do what Godwall says! All the People of all the Lands must do exactly what Godwall dictates. It is our true Deity. We don't need to know why it makes demands. We must only believe with total Faith that It knows best.

She hesitated, then learned forward, a quick suggestion of desire flaring once again in those clear, clean blue, passionately expressive eyes.

Was it his imagination? Did she want him to draw her close, crush those perfect lips against his own? Was she silently pleading for him to overwhelm her resistant with his strong male lust? Would she even resist? Or want to? Surely no princess in her right mind would entertain such wicked thoughts.

For a moment longer those eyes seemed to burn with fiery passion. Then quickly, as if cut away by some wizard's magic, the bright, hot flame flickered out.

He wasn't even sure what passions had been reflected in her longing gaze. Since it simply wasn't possible for a Princess of such quality to even imagine such animal desires, it must have merely been a fantasy illusion created in his perversely passion-sick mind.

When he remained frozen, unmoving, she drew back, and coldly stated: "The People hardly know what is best of them. That's what we have Laws for,

28

customs...rules. It would be horrid to do something that Godwall said was wrong. Just horrid!"

He was still warring with his almost overwhelming urge to drag her close. Golter's advice concerning the making of maidens was ripping at his guts. How he envied the Common Folk; envied Golter and his maiden. He wanted to cover this lovely young Princess' face with passionate kisses. He wanted that almost more than winning Status and Fame.

Her mood suddenly changed, as was the habit of females in the lands. A man could never guess what they might say or do next. The Princess was turning hot, then cold, then sad and warm. Such mood swings were quite confusing; they all seemed to circle back on one another, mixing and folding, blending together into a shatteringly forceful pattern of conflicting emotions. Women could be so difficult! How did a man ever know what was truly expected of him? Believe the words or the silent—and perhaps miss—read messages?

"Oh, Mhyo, I may never see you—" Her voice choked with real anguish.

They stood there for several moments saying nothing, then all at once, seemingly totally out of context, she asked: "You don't love me enough to—"

"What?"

"Well...to...you know. Surely you know how I feel."

"I can't read your mind."

"But my wishes. My desires. Surely you know...you must know." The frustration was raw in her voice. It was obvious that he wasn't getting some unspoken message. And the Princess was becoming more and more annoyed by that fact. "If you loved me enough to—"

"To...what?"

"Don't you know? Can't you guess?"

"Come on. I'd do anything. Anything you ask. Just ask!"

Would it be for a kiss? The thought clutched at the sides of his skull, which now throbbed with wanton desire. Did she want to be kissed?

Or something? Maybe even more?

Impossible!

"If you must be asked, well then I ask you to..." She only looked away. Thus hiding the expression on her face. "Well...to...do what Godwall says!"

Somehow he felt that really wasn't what she had wanted to say.

The young Princess moved towards the exit to the garden, starting for the large wooden door that led to her very private chambers. Even her father had never been beyond that point.

She pointed with her arm, dramatically extended, contemptuously demanding with her eyes. "Find out from Deathwall the secret of what you are and maybe then you will have learned how to become a true and honest and worthy Warrior—maybe Deathwall can teach you something about true conquest and how to claim your well earned rewards. You...oh, never mind!"

The young woman turned and for a moment stood at the entrance to her rooms, then said over her shoulder: "I don't want to see you again until you have discovered what you are. Or that you are more than you are...what ever Godwall said. Go. A

30

Princess waits only so long for her man to become worthy of her."

With that final statement, Princess Ginnia opened the large wooden door. Then she disappeared into her chambers.

He experienced a feeling of dejected, confusion. It had actually almost seemed as if she had somehow been offering entrance to her private chambers. Of course that had to be imagination fired by his hotly perverse desires.

Damn Golter for his rotting advice. Common Folks were such crude people. Damn him again.

But, then, maybe there was more to her words than their form suggested. Perhaps it wasn't his imagination. Perhaps women, maiden or Princess, truly wanted the same thing men desired. Perhaps Golter had been right. Perhaps even a Princess wanted to be know in a carnal way.

But a Warrior was defined to protect all maidens common or Royal. Even from their own wicked, overwhelming, most human and enjoyable, desires. Even from themselves.

Nevertheless, a kiss might not have been too much to offer him. She could have kissed him good-bye.

Frustrated by such thoughts, tormented by the longing power of his passions, he turned and left the garden of the Princess.

THE SNAKE MONSTER SPEAKS

[Editorial note: At this point much of the text is garbled, incomplete or next to meaningless. There were many adventures hinted at, but not detailed enough to relate here. While of interest to historians, such fragments have no place here, other than to indicate that a lot of details were lost in Time. There were hundreds of incomplete lines that survived, alone, isolated, such as: "Mhyo sank his lance into the side of the Koakia Monster." "... lopping off one of its ugly, huge green heads with his sword..." These are surely intriguing, but nothing more. There were half scenes, partial events, none complete enough to be a part of this present publication. But they do suggest that much happened, at least of a minor nature, during this time frame. It is enough to note here that, apparently, our young Warrior gained some practical experience in fighting, hunting and surviving. As usual we have used the [...] to indicated missing parts.]

There had been more and more signs posted along the road, as they crossed the Land of Walls. They announced: "Dangerous Snake." "Snake of Forked Tongue." "Beware of the Fire-Breathing Snake." For the most part they were unnoticed by our two friends.

[...]

"Did you see that?" Golter wanted to know, pointing up above the hills to the East of them. "That bird?"

Mhyo nodded. "I've seen the Kioa bird before."

"Of course you have. We've been eating them almost daily. But the sign it was carrying in its beak."

"No, I didn't see it."

"Hey!" Golter yelled, "Here come another one."

Mhyo's eyes followed the direction of the other's frantically pointing hand.

Flying right across their path, high in the sky, was the huge Kioa bird, its monstrous leathered wings flapping gracefully through the air. From its thick neck hung a large purple banner flaying in the wind.

"Be warned of the mighty power of the Snake that Speaks!"

"What," Mhyo wondered, "do you make of that?"

Golter slowly shook his head, like a dazed frog. "Don't know. But I have seen a couple of small signs posted along the road. Think this snake might be a dragon?"

"A snake is surely a snake. The label defines. A snake isn't a dragon...I don't think. That is, unless it was a very Big snake. Then it might be considered a small dragon."

"You could kill a small dragon...even a Big one!"

"Why? For food?"

"You are a Mighty Warrior that must kill his required number of Dragons. Didn't the Princess tell you that.?"

"Yes. I'm required, as the Warrior's Manual of Arts and Rewards so dictates, to kill a certain number of Dragons in order to win her hand."

"And I would hope more than that," Golter offered, an evil grin on his face.

"Her heart and mind and soul," Mhyo agreed.

"And a lot more than that," Golter persisted.

"Well, anyway..."

"Anyway my foot. You can kill a Dragon or two—"

"If I can find one."

"A snake seems like a likely target," Golter suggested. "At least a beginning."

"I don't know." Mhyo sounded uncertain, as he directed his horse down the pathway to a shadowy meadow below. The afternoon sky was darkening, and soon they would have to stop for the night. "A snake would hardly be..."

[...]

It was early morning, the sun radiating down through the thickly laced intertwining branches of the huge forest trees. Mhyo and Golter moved carefully down the narrow pathway that led to the pool of the Speaking Snake. There was a sign nicely posted on the side of the road with the neatly printed words:

SPEAKING SNAKE AHEAD

Above the sign was a blinking red neon that warned:

34

Beware! Beware! Danger Ahead!

Finally they turned a bend and came to the sudden break in the forest. Now they found themselves facing a huge stagnant pool, rippling slightly as if some silent invisible god were breathing upon its slimy green surface.

The weathered wooden sign was crudely nailed to a stake that was driven deeply into the bank near the edge of the water. The lettering was brushed on in white:

STAGNANT POOL

To drink of these waters could be dangerous to your health.

Smoking, of course, is Forbidden!

Golter remained safely behind his master, totally uncertain; as usual. What might seem cowardly was nothing more than a realistic lack of confidence in a very limited fighting ability. He accepted Mhyo's skill in battle to be good enough for both of them; plus the natural hesitation built into his own rank and file. After all, he was a man servant. Nothing more, nothing less. How could he be anything else? The gods had made him thus; and thus he had fully matured to his present state. (And, after all, being a crude servant had its advantages, insofar as the enjoyment of the maiden sect. He pitied the Warrior's Ethical Code that denied enjoyment of such carnal pleasures.)

Mhyo, for his part, was grim-faced, ready for battle. sword drawn, shield gripped tightly in front of him. He was even anxious to have the chance to slay a dragon, as was expected of him.

The rippling of the water grew more obvious, as if some disruption were taking place under its surface. Then, with a frightening lunge and loud hiss, a monstrous creature lifted up from the pool; its fangs exposed, eyes glaring dangerously at the two men on horseback. Green slime dripped from its thin lips.

"Who is this that comes bothering my resting place?" the snake roared furiously at Mhyo, pointedly ignoring what was so obviously nothing more dangerous than a mere servant, cringing behind the magnificent warrior.

Mhyo held up his shield to block a deadly attack, gripped the broadsword firmly in his large right hand, balanced so that it could swing forward in a counter-attack, if that proved possible.

Golter held his horse tightly under control as it attempted to rebel in fear.

"A Warrior!" Mhyo shouted back, feeling quite small compared to this giant serpent head swinging slowly back and forth a mere ten terrible feet above him.

"You don't have to shout!" the snake cried, drawing its head way back.. "My ears may not be obvious, but I have outstanding hearing. You can believe that. You can."

Golter had to fight the urge to flee, let his horse take control and retreat up the hill. This snake was huge, monstrous, overwhelming, a living, breathing skyscraper that kept swaying back and forth above them.

For a long moment the snake said nothing more. It just watched them. The creature seemed to be attempting to decide what kind of threat these small puny human creatures could offer; or, maybe, more realistically, what kind of morning snack the two might make. The golden sun outlined the fine thick coils, as wide as Mhyo's body, light flared on the slimy scales.

Shaking its head, the snake seemed to slowly drift out of some strangely hypnotic daze, or, perhaps, merely awaken from a deep sleep. Slowly that face lowered down towards the two men, eyes glaring at Mhyo.

"Oh, so you are a Warrior," the snake mused. "Come to kill dragons, no doubt."

"Well, if necessary."

The snake's head lifted. Those huge eyes blinked rapidly; the gaping mouth yawned, then said: "Yes...that is what Warriors seem to hunger for: dragon killing. Yes. A Warrior and his servant. Yes. True and terrifying. I assume. To say the least, I might add. For sure. So. You are a Warrior. Very fine. A highly desirable career, if you ask me. But what else have you done with your fine young life besides being a Warrior?"

"I...well, I have fallen in love."

"Oh, love. Yes. Fine. Fine. That is pure delight. And what else have you done in your young life?

"I...I went before Godwall."

The snaked coiled, hissing, furiously retreated into the sky, exposed his fangs and snarled. That five-forked tongue danced rapidly out, vibrating. Those huge, monstrous eyes, the size of a maiden's face, seemed to sink into the folds of its yellow and purple skin.

This show of raw terror seemed to give Golter courage. He now came up beside Mhyo, though carefully cringing in a blatant show of what seemed to be the required respect.

"Oh, terrible. Oh, that is terrible!" the snake hissed, as if in some kind of snake-coughing spasm. "Terrible."

"What's wrong with Godwall?" Mhyo demanded, defensively, still holding bravely onto the broadsword; ready for anything.

"What is wrong with Godwall? You don't know?" the snake hissed in mockery. "You have seen Godwall and you do not know? But...come to think of it, of course, how could you know? How could a mere Warrior—a grand title and a grand career, I do admit—know what is wrong with Godwall?

The snake uncoiled slowly, letting its long, thick purple rattle disappear into the slimy green of the filth infested pond.

"What is so wrong with Godwall?" Mhyo demanded.

"Come to think of it I imagine there is nothing wrong with any of the Walls—if you look at it in that manner. A Wall is a Wall. And they are all just fine Walls, they surely are."

Golter spoke up for the first time. "Well, that's the right way to look at it."

"Right or wrong, left or right, back and forth, curl or not, circles and circles of words and ideas. All are directions one might take; any of which might offer the path one would pick to follow. If one wanted to pick a path to follow...that is. Though, of course, any path is as good as another; for they all lead to Deathwall. Some more directly, some more confusingly, but in the end you always reach Deathwall—unless, of course, you turn around and go backwards—and you wouldn't do that on purpose. And all the People have great and grand purpose, so they seldom go backwards, all of which is of little importance to me, come to think of it."

Once again the snake coiled in on itself, sinking a little deeper into the green slime that was its home. "As for me, I would rather enjoy myself right here. It is safer, you know."

Then, as if by afterthought, it added: "That is...you aren't planning on killing me, are you?"

"Is that an option?" Mhyo wondered, as if surprised the snake would admit to such a possibility.

"I would hope not! I certainly would hope not. I'd rather enjoy myself right here, in my slimy depths, than do battle to the death with a fine young Warrior like yourself."

Then, as if by afterthought, it added: "That is...you aren't really planning on killing me, are you?"

"Why? Should I?"

"Well that is your career, is it not? It defines you. Killing. Your...well, if you wish, profession...that to which you have dedicated your life. This killing. At least I thought all normal Warriors were out to slay dragons and to kill. And, well, I would imagine you might think me a dragon if you did not look close enough, or hadn't read all the road signs along the way. If you look close enough—and who really looks all that close? At anybody. At anything? Especially at snakes?

"I'm merely on my way to see Deathwall."

"Oh?" Mention of that Deity seemed to bring just the suggestion of a contented smile on its slimy lips. "Why? Why do you wish to seek Deathwall?"

"To answer the question Godwall gave me."

"What question?"

"Well, It said that Deathwall will tell me the answer to how to become more than I am."

"Why that's easy: eat a lot!"

"That is one way," Mhyo admitted.

"Ridiculous!" Golter muttered, now more at ease. Even a servant could see how silly the conversation had become.

"But it is an answer," Mhyo quickly offered, soothingly. Though he shrugged his shoulders, as if in agreement with Golter.

"But not the right answer?" The snake looked honestly puzzled. Those large eyes crossed dramatically; huge fanged mouth gaped wide enough to gobble a human body in one swallow. "When I eat a lot my body swells. I become a larger snake. I...bulge all over. But, then, of course, after I've digested the creature, I end up being the same snake I was before. More or less. That is."

Mhyo shrugged, but said nothing.

"Of course, that's not the right answer!" Golter retorted in a bold voice. He was quite obviously feeling boulder, having survived these first few moments without any harm befalling him. Furthermore, from his practical servant's eyes and ears, it was apparent that this was just a foolish reptile. "You stupid snake!"

The snake pointedly chose to ignore the insult.

"I guess you are right. Godwall would not consider that a very good answer; at least, not the right—or left—one. Well, anyway, it considers very few things to be real and true answers. Godwall, so I've been told, speaks in riddles that have no real meaning at all. Well...no apparent meaning. I suppose. None to me. Anyway.

"But...well...these Riddles. They're meaningless Riddles. If you ask me." Somehow the snake looked as if it had shrugged; of course, that had to be an illusion, since it had no shoulders to shrug with. Nonetheless it seemed to shrug.

"Maybe that is why he sent you to Deathwall. On the other hand, maybe he sent you to Deathwall because you are stupid; like all the People and all Warriors. Or simply because this is where you will, finally, end, if you follow any of the paths. Unless, of course, you were to go backwards to Godwall. But he would then simply rescind you along the way you came. Thus, I'm afraid, you would be going backward...once again. Or...would it be forward? It all does become very confusing in the end. Except when you face Deathwall. Well, so I'm told. But I have never seen Deathwall and have no desire to do so and so I stay here, safe, where no dangers can seek me out—well, very few. I have found it necessary to enjoy a maiden or Warrior in my Time, but that is another issue. Today, I'm not hungry. And that is fine for you—and for me."

"Oh?" Mhyo felt suddenly amused.

Golter's horse backed slightly away.

"Why of course. Otherwise I would have simply eaten both of you."

"If I let you," Mhyo laughed a bit brazenly.

"What could you do?"

"Kill you."

"Yes, my master would kill you. He surely would kill you. Kill you! Kill, like totally, completely dead, chopped up and fried, cooked into patties and fed to the...well, you would be good meat for those who like snakes. I guess. Anyway. You'd be dead, quick and simple, for my master is a fine and wonderful Warrior. So. There!"

"Yes, that is a possibility. A slim one. But a very strange possibility since no Warrior has come my way who could kill me—at least I'm not dead, yet. Am I? No. I'm certainly not dead. Otherwise I would not be talking to you. But, that is interesting. You think you could kill me?"

"I am trained to kill and I have survived many battles on my why here. I probably could kill you. I was trained to kill all that might face me in honest and honorable battle."

"What about dishonest and dishonorable battle?"

"That would be—well...cheating. I mean—"

"You mean that it is okay to kill when it is honorable and honest but it is cheating and wicked and murder to kill when it is the other way around."

"Something like that."

Golter broke in with: "Of course. My master kills only in honorable battle. It is the only honorable way to kill."

"Some powers and forces do not agree with you. I'm certain that Deathwall would not agree. But, then, Deathwall has its own sense of morality and that is simply to be destructive for the pleasure of destruction." The snake snapped to attention as if some unseen threat might be near, but its words shook that illusion away. "Why, of course, you are a

Warrior and you surely must consider Deathwall your true deity."

"Godwall is our Deity," Golter spoke for both of them.

"But you are trained to kill, Warrior, to be a destroyer. And this...well...this speaking servant is—well, never mind. Would it not be logical to automatically offer your services to Deathwall? Maybe that is what Godwall meant when It said to seek your answer there about how to become something other than you are."

"No. Godwall said to become more than I am."

"Well, quibble with words it you wish, but I won't. That is the way of Speaking Walls. Who ever heard of Speaking Walls, anyway? It does not make sense, when you think of it."

"Nor do speaking snakes!" Golter observed, nastily.

"Quite right. Or speaking People. Speaking, in itself, is silly."

"It communicates ideas," Mhyo suggested, still finding this conversation a bit amusing.

"Ideas are silly."

Golter, a bit needled and confused, found himself nodding in dumb agreement.

"Why?" Mhyo demanded. "Why are ideas silly?"

"Because your idea of an idea is different from my idea of an idea. See? Plus we are probably both wrong about our ideas in the first place. So it is all silliness in the last place. Which could be the first place. That is if you go backwards."

Golter shook his head in total confusion, as if trying to rid it of loose water on the brain.

Mhyo simply asked: "Why is it that I some how get the impression that everybody I speak to is talking in circles, always returning to the same point?"

The snake smiled, if that was possible for a snake to do.

"Yes, why? Why?" Golter anxiously offered..

"If I knew I probably would not tell you. And if I did not know I probably would act as if I did know but was not willing to tell you. Which all means the same thing, no matter in which direction you look at it."

"Why wouldn't you tell us?" Mhyo asked as Golter groaned.

"I could ask: Why should I tell you? But I won't. I won't say, either, that this is what you must learn for yourself—if anybody were to tell you, you would have to take their word for it. But what if you are the kind of Warrior who did not like taking another's word for something? Then you would not believe. Thus, in the end, you would have to find out for yourself. So it is easier not to tell you even if I know. And, of course, if I do not know, I simply must act as if I did know and am not willing to tell you."

"Why?" Golter fairly screamed, revealing his total anger and frustration. "Why would you do that?"

"Well, even a snake does not like to be thought of as being anything less than a snake. And if the two of you have a low profile on snakes, well, that's your problem; but my problem is to at least give you the impression that I am something more than I am. In that way I can feel I am thought of, at the very least, as being exactly what I am."

44

"Why not be what you are: honest and open. Just tell us the truth?" Mhyo suggested, for the first time a bit angry.

"Why not be something I am not so that you will think I am not what I am—or what I am, I'm not? I'm a snake. Did you ever know a snake that would tell you everything wanted to know?"

"Even Godwall would not—"

"Ah. See? And you wish me to be better than Godwall? Flattering. I think. How flattering."

Golter glance at Mhyo, silently pleading, as the Warrior said: "I only wish you would be less confusion."

"I am less confusion than you are. You are very much confusion—and confusing. You are a Warrior and yet you seek Deathwall. Why? Because Godwall told you to? And why? Just to discover if you are—correction: can be, or how to be—something other, or more, than you are? That does not make sense because nobody can be something they are not."

"We change!" Golter blurted.

Mhyo said: "If we change we become something else. That is quite and totally impossible. We are what we are, nothing more."

Golter shook his head in disgust.

The snake quickly licked its lips. "Unless a wizard or witch decides to do something horrible to us like changing a snake into a staff and a staff into a snake. But that is magic. And I do not, for quite obvious reasons, like to believe in magic. If I did I would be a different snake. I like being the snake I am. Though, of course, I don't mind making others think I am a different snake than I am—but that is another matter."

"You don't change, but you like to be something you are not!" Golter groaned, but this time Mhyo thought he heard the hint of mocking in his servant's voice.

"I like being what I am, I simply do not always want others to know what that is. Or, if they have a low profile of snakes I find it necessary to impress them with my wisdom. Thus they can gain a better impression of me. In such a manner they can start believing that a snake is more than they thought it was in the first place."

"Is that the way to become more than you are?" Mhyo now inquired a bit too seriously. "Simply by making others think you are something you aren't?"

"You talk like a fool! Not a Warrior. Well, correction. You talk like a Warrior; and a Warrior might be a fool acting like he is a Warrior. In such a manner he would thus appear to be impressive to others. Others, of course, who were uneducated enough not to understand the difference. If there is a difference, that is. On the other hand, he would simply confuse others so completely they will not know the fool is less than the Warrior—which he wants to be. But you are quite obviously a Warrior. So—there!"

"You did not answer my question."

"Did I promise to ever answer any of your questions?"

"No."

"Then I have not broken my promise."

"Nor did you promise not to answer—" Golter blurted, as if having made a wonderful discovery and delighted in bringing up the point.

"That is correct."

"You did not even make a promise," Mhyo offered, feeling as if having been conned.

"How true. And if one does not make a promise they do not have to worry about breaking it."

"It is talking double talk!" Golter complained.

The young Warrior nodded, said: "I do somehow get the impression this conversation is getting nowhere."

"Nowhere, somewhere. All leads to Deathwall. Unless you go backwards. Which leads to Godwall. But of course he will only send you forward to Deathwall. Thus you will be backtracking, once again. And you won't know if you are going backwards or forward, coming or going. You will, thus, end up more confused than you were in the beginning. So continue your journey and let sleeping snakes sleep—or if you wait much longer I just might get hungry and it will be necessary to eat you alive."

For a moment Mhyo stared at the snake, aware of the fact that so far in his journey he had killed no real dragons. He considered the idea of entering into battle with this snake. After all, he was a dragon slayer. It was a great temptation. But then, he realized, a snake was not a dragon. Most of all, this snake had, regardless of all else, served as a kind of perverse amusement. If nothing else. He was not so certain that what the snake had said made any kind of sense, but the fact remained it did not openly challenge him to combat. To attack an enemy without cause would hardly be very honorable.

Finally, without another word, Mhyo turned his horse around. Golter quickly followed.

For a moment it seemed that the snake was about to do exactly as it had threatened, devour them as an afternoon snack.

As the two men spurred their mounts once again in the direction they had been told was the shortest route to Deathwall, both were silent, puzzled by their encounter with the Speaking Snake.

They blindly passed the sign that read:

SHORT ROUTE 666 TO DEATHWALL

They had noticed too many of these kinds of signs to pay any attention to them. They didn't even notice the neon light that flashed on and off in the distance:

YOUNG WIZARD AHEAD!

Magic, Magic, Magic!"

YOUNG WIZARD OF "GREAT" MAGIC

There it was, bright in its multicolored letters:

MAGIC

Wonderful Magic of All Kinds
It had floated in front of them. They seldom noticed, for they were simply out of phase with the neon sign. Our two companions had other problems, like hunting for food, fighting off real nightmares. And searching for Dragons.

They had broken camp just before dawn, after a very generous breakfast of boiled Snou-eggs and Mio-Meat. Both men felt contented, and, of course, expected nothing unusual to take place as they continued their journey through the woods

It all happened. Rather fast.

They came upon the wizard quite unexpectedly. The trees had thinned out to reveal an open plane. It was then that they saw the young man standing on a large flat gray boulder.

The Mountains of Zint lifted high into the afternoon sky; their snow-capped peaks showing boldly in the distance. He just stood there against this magnificent backdrop of Nature, facing them. His arms waved grandly in the air as if in worship of the blue sky or some invisible, nature god. He was very young—in fact even younger than our two adventurers. No beard marred his childlike face. Yet there was a quality of deep, penetrating Smarts in his green eyes.

Mhyo stopped his horse right in front of the man, then glanced at Golter, who shrugged in puzzled response.

The young man's black, deep-set eyes seemed to be staring directly at them, yet it took several moments before he saw these newcomers.

Suddenly his head shook, then he grinned.

"Well, hello." Those arms continued to move, robe flying in the air around him.

"Hello," Mhyo countered, dismounting.

Golter asked: "What are you doing?"

"Being a great wizard."

"I mean, well, what are you, well...er...wizzing?"

"My special brand of magic. My own...thing...well, Art. Kinda doing it my way. Frankly speaking I think it's kinda Great Stuff. My thing...my Art, that is."

Mhyo sat on the gold speckled rock that lay only a few feet from the tall, young man. He silently considered what had been said.

Doing your own "thing" sounded quit dated. Decades ago the People had tried that as a Social Experiment—with terrible results. Godwall's New Laws returned structure and sanity. Too many People doing their "thing" had, so Godwall claimed, brought moral decay. Values dropped like a dead Stock Market report, so the Grand and Mighty Godwall proclaimed. But then It was, by Nature, quite conservative.

"And what," Mhyo wanted to know, "exactly is your, well, thing?"

"Well," came the ready answer, "right now doing this."

They watched in silence, waiting for something to happen. But nothing vanished, nothing appeared, nothing changed. Everything was oblivious of any Thing happening.

The young wizard merely stood there waving his arms.

"What do you think?" Golter whispered to Mhyo.

"I don't know. Seems kinda silly to me."

The arms came crashing down. "Silly? What are you whispering about? I resent that."

Those hands slapped to his narrow hips. "I'm a great wizard. Even if you must—because of my age—spell it with a small w. And what might seem nothing to you is something very important to me."

"And what," Mhyo wanted to know, "would that be?

"What's important to me is IMPORTANT! See?"

"Yes, but I meant what is your age? You are rather young to be a wizard."

"Perhaps. But I'm older than I look."

"As old as fifteen to seventeen?"

"I'm much older. I was around when you were a Daddy's gleam-in-the-eye-dream. But never mind that. I am, of course, no doubt about it, very young for a wizard. And that's enough for you to know."

Mhyo decided to ignore that last quip.

It was Golter who leaped to his feet, his sword clanking as he waved his arms wildly in the air in mocking movements. He appeared to be an awkward frog, jerking back and forth, thick muscular arms flexing and flying up and down, legs bending and dipping.

When there was no verbal reaction, though Mhyo covered his lips to repress a smile, Golter stopped, breathing hard.

"What was all that about?" The wizard's voice was ice cold.

"Don't you know? I was doing my thing!"

"Funny, funny, funny. Very, very funny. Indeed. I'm doubling over in convulsions." There was no sign of humor on the young wizard's face. Instead he glared at Golter as if the man servant were a bug to be merely crushed.

"But I like waving my arms," Golter stated, though he was grinning.

"Mockery is a fool profession. But then, I guess you are a good fool, Golter."

"How'd you know my name?"

"I know many things. You are a servant of this Warrior Mhyo Janton. You brag about carnal delights with the maiden sect. You think maidens are to be...made. So clever that pause. So grand. So cute...but primitive. So cheap. You go directly for the carnal trade. Maids for Sale. Hot, passionate females. Willing, wanton broads. Right to Go—"

"I sure do!" came the eager reply.

"Well, that's your thing."

"My thing! For sure. And three halves!" Golter puffed up like an over bloated frog. "Maybe three and a half halves."

"Make that 10,000 and a half. Perhaps to the N half!" The wizard shrugged, dismissing such numbers as meaningless. "That's just find. If you say so."

"I say so. So. There! At least my pleasures are normal to the normal Folk. We might be common, but we enjoy life. We do normal things the normal way. That's why we are called..."

"Normal? Common?"

"At least I'm...not...waving my arms in the air like a foolish—"

"Stop! Right there! Don't mock others simply because you don't understand what they are doing."

Mhyo, quite serious, suggested; "Why don't you tell us what you are really doing?"

"Great magic. Of course," the wizard retorted, annoyed. "Natch!" and wizard-fingers snapped. "Like that." The fingers snapped again. "Light a match!" The wizard looked at them, grinning. "Natch. Like that. Light a match."

That hand waved madly in the air, as if on fire. And for a glimmering moment it seemed a glow radiated out from their tips.

"See?" the wiz asked, extending his arm, so they could more easily observe those fingers. "See them? "We see," Golter shrugged, "Nothing."

"You don't see anything happening? No Flaming Fingers?" The wiz sounded puzzled, now looking at the Warrior. "Well. that was really nothing but a parlor trick."

Golter, with arms crossed angrily on his barrel chest, demand:. "What trick?"

"Snap, snap!" The wizard's fingers clicked loudly together. "Natch. Like that. Light a match."

Mhyo had now also crossed his arms. He watched with a sense of amusement. Waiting.

"Anything?" the wiz inquired, almost pleading. The wizard frowned, then shook his hand violently.

There was just the suggestion of light on the tips of the young man's fingers. But that was surely a trick of lighting. Mhyo shrugged that off as Sun Illusion.

Golter merely sat there, as if the wizard had turned him to stone.

"Oh well. That was one parlor gag I could never get right, anyway. But...the other thing...Surely when you approached me you saw the great magic I was experiencing."

Warrior and servant alike shook their heads firmly from side to side.

"You have eyes. Did you not see me waving my arms in the air?"

They both sat there without moving, just staring blankly at the young wizard.

"Well, that's great magic."

"I don't understand." Mhyo's eyes leveled with the other's.

"Do you have to understand?

"We would like to," the young Warrior admitted.

"Then...well okay. Stand. Wave your arms. As I do. Come, come. Do it. Then maybe you will understand. Do as I say! After all, only through experience can one understand anything at all."

"What will happen?" Golter wanted to know.

"Try. And discover." Those eyes, turning a deep gold, challenged him. "Come, come. Stand!"

Reluctantly, they stood.

"Now do as I do! Come. Come, come, come! Do it." The wizard lifted his arms in the air, made a wide circle with them.

The two followed his example. For some minutes they moved their arms in the same manner as the wizard, following complicated patterns, all the time expecting something to happen. Anything. Nothing did. Of course.

Mhyo finally lowered his arms. Golter, thankfully, followed that example.

The wizard froze. "Well, do you see, now?

"No!" Golter exclaimed in contempt.

"Not at all," Mhyo merely observed, curious.

"Then you will never see, no doubt."

"Why not explain, then?" Mhyo pressed, really interested in knowing what the young wizard was talking about.

"Simple. The magic is in the joy of doing what you wish to do, no matter what that is."

"But that's not productive," Golter observed.

"Does it have to be?" the wizard demanded of Mhyo, ignoring the servant.

Mhyo thought, then offered; "It is supposed to be. Godwall demands all to be productive. Warriors War, Kings King, Gods God and the People are productive."

"Where does it say in the Big Sky Above that we must be productive in a manner that all understand? To me this is productive!" Seeing that the two men did not understand, the wizard continued: "It exercises my arms, if nothing more. And exercise is suppose to be good for you. Even Godwall would understand that!"

Golter leaned aggressively forward. "We get exercise enough!"

Mhyo agreed. "It would be a foolish...er...exercise to exercise that way."

The wizard looked puzzled. "I thought all the People were fat, lazy, watching the local Sitcoms and Plays and feeding their faces with fried foods of wizard-parts and not exercising enough. Aren't the Exercise Tapes popular with the People?"

Golter moaned, muttered to Mhyo, "Can you believe this guy? He's talking about the Health Club Racket. Only the rich can afford that."

Before Mhyo could reply, the wizard shrugged that away with: "I can't be bothered keeping up with the Pop Trends. I have better ways to waist my Time."

Golter's face looked like he had eaten fiery peppers. "You're full of it. And full of yourself!" The servant's voice grew louder as he spoke, until he was fairly screaming. "You do nothing but wave your arms in the air. That's nothing. Nothing. Nothing! It simply is NOT productive!"

"You think it has to be?"

Both men nodded.

The wizard responded by lifting his right hand, palm to them, then clicking off the fingers one at a time, to illustrate each point:

"It makes pretty patterns in the air that I can see, because I am sensitive enough to see them."

Finger One seemed to flicker, disappeared.

"It pleases me, like a great work of art, one that continues to move and amaze.

Finger Two faded.

"I can see light patterns reflecting in the atoms as they are sparked into life by the movements of my arms."

Finger Three flashed out of existence.

"His hand!" Golter cried. "Where'd they go?"

"Real Magic creates a sensual art that is highly rewarding."

The two men were wide-eyed as they stared at that now almost defingered hand.

What magic had done that? Mhyo silently wondered. Real or Illusion? Really only a parlor trick or true magic? Perhaps this young wizard really could wiz a trick or two. Or... The wizard frowned at the one finger and thumb remaining on his hand. A moment of silence followed as if he were trying to understand something. Then he shook the hand, and suddenly, as if by magic, the fingers flashed into place, one at a time. "It is all a rewarding exercise. To me. At least. And that should be enough. For me. Anyway."

Golter and Mhyo looked wide-eyed at the now totally whole hand.

"Oh, that. Simply parlor stuff. Mere illusion Fakery. A trick. See?" The hand waved and the fingers flashed away, then came suddenly back into place. "Tricks a kid in pre-school might do."

Golter moaned. "I don't know no kids who did that kind of thing."

"Nobody who belonged to the local Magic Club?'

"Nothing."

"And you, find Warrior?"

"No."

"Godwall! Where have you been all your lives?"

"Obviously," Golter muttered, "not running in the same circles you are."

"Circles...? Ha! I see you've paid the required visit to that Snake of the Slimy Pool."

"How'd you know?" Golter sounded stunned.

"Circles. Circles. Circles. All are circles to It because It coils in on itself. Got me?"

Golter rapidly shook his head.

Mhyo quickly explained: "I think my friend here meant that neither of us ran around in that kind of social circle. I mean, with the kids that liked magic tricks."

"You missed a lot."

Golter snapped: "What? No foolishness with us. None of that kid stuff. We had to learn how to survive."

"Oh, yeah. Hard work and all that. Foolish effort for little gain. There are better ways to survive. Wit. And Brains. Use a quick tongue."

"So you are a con wiz?" Golter suggested.

"I am what I am. And I do great magic, believe it or not!"

"But we don't see it," Mhyo boldly challenged.

"Yeah, yeah," Golter agreed. "Seeing is believing. No see, no joy."

"How many great masterworks of art have fools found valueless, simply because they do not have the senses to enjoy? A picture of a lovely, seductive, smiling maid might hide the truth she's a mean spirited demon! How do we know the artist's true message? Or the real Nature of the model? We think of her as a Madonna, but does that make her so?

"The title defines," Mhyo argued.

"Yes, so I heard. Art is Art. It can mean almost anything. Because it is Art—not Reality. And Art reflects the artist's Reality. The art might show a Terrible Rex, that could be a lizard or Dragon, or merely the imaginary idea of the Artist. What you see ain't always what you get! So seeing is not always believing. If you have the Smarts to know the difference. Or the imagination to...well...imagine the different."

The wizard signed, continued: "It is not important that others enjoy. If you enjoy the Art, that is nice. Fine. Okay with me. Some see, some don't. We all see with different degrees of understanding. Many of the People will mock us more creative types. Let them. I only care that my purpose and meaning is important to me." The wizard poked his chest. "I don't care if you see or not. If I see Lizards, you might see Dragons."

Golter groused: "Where's the dragons? We haven't seen no dragons."

"You want to see one?" the wiz asked, a bit surprised.

"No. I don't. Just him. The Warrior One."

"Yes, he would, wouldn't he?"

"Yes," Mhyo agreed, "he would. The required amount of...you know...stuff."

"Dragons—say it!" Golter moaned. "The guy is obsessed with Dragons."

Mhyo merely shrugged that off.

The wiz asked: "What kind of Dragons would please you?"

Golter was quick to answer that one: "The fire-breathing, skyscraper kind. With big jaws that'll swallow huge buildings in a single gulp. Claws as big as a man's arm. Teeth as sharp as—"

"Oh, yes. The normal, mail-order, run-in-the-mill Terrible Rex. The everyday, ordinary kind of, easy to recognize, Dragon of Ol'. Certainly, the obvious Dragon with sharp teeth."

"Didn't I say that?" Golter muttered, almost angrily. "You can conjure up that kind of monster?"

"Well I don't bother with that kind of conjuring."

Golter whispered: "He just cons in a different way, if you ask me. Pure con...delight."

"I heard that," the wiz stated in a matter-of-fact manner. "But you see, though you obviously don't see...the magic I make is for myself, alone. If others do see, I have no objections. I'm really quite generous. Look and enjoy, if you must, I care not, one way or the other. I like my magic...Art. I value it."

"You can't eat that kind of stuff. What about the necessities of life." Golter wanted to know.

"Food? Piff! What's so magic about that?"

"Everybody has to have food in order to eat," Golter fairly yelled.

"I have my ways..."

"Conjuring or...begging?" Golter countered with contempt.

"I offer a Service, from Time to Time. There is always a way to get a meal."

"I suppose," the loyal servant admitted, having, himself, managed more than once to swipe a dish. Especially of the female type. "But on a daily basis?"

"Some folk are wiser, smarter, luckier than others. Everybody survives, one way or another—or they die. Living is the art of surviving. So there."

Mhyo said, "I suppose...you're right about that last part. But...Golter is right, too."

"If you wish. Still, I have great magic that feeds my spirit."

"Well, " Mhyo pointedly stated, "we normal folk—"

"Normal compared to whom? I consider you subnormal, for you have less senses than I. Though some would consider you supernormal, because they have no sense. It is all depends on your POV. Just don't mock others for what they experience. If I wave my arms in the air, I get LifeMagic. Even if others can not see my Art, or simply consider it Trashy, doesn't effect its true value. Understand?"

"Don't you really care what others think?" Mhyo countered.

Golter added: "You got to do what is expected. That is the Law. Godwall—"

"Godwall. All I hear from People is what Godwall says. Or what Deathwall threatens or does. Who cares? They don't effect me. Anyway, the People are fools!"

"But," Mhyo offered.

"But nothing. I enjoy my Art. The reward is in myself—it feeds me, its gives me life, subsistence. And I am filled with this wondrous Food."

"Strange food," Golter muttered out of the side of his mouth.

The wizard looked disgusted. "Frogs eat insects!"

"What does that have to do—"

61

"Merely points out one of the ways frogs survive."

"You aren't a frog?" Mhyo laughed.

"I'm not you. Either. Or you. Or anything other than myself. I grow and feed on my experience."

Both of them looked at the young wizard, without saying a word. After a moment the wizard continued.

"Look at you...what gives you pleasure? Ask yourself that. No. Don't bother me with your Q&As on the subject. We should do only what gives us pleasure. Why embrace another's life style? Don't follow the other guy's trail. Remember what the Wise Ol' Snake said: All roads lead...etc. etc. Let the People do what turns on their lights."

The wiz hesitated, then considered the sky. "Come to think of it, we need all the lights turned on. Without Light we could hardly see."

Golter leaped to his feet, stabbing a beefy finger towards the wizard. "See, there is a grand reason for us common Folk. We keep the light burning!"

"Yes, that's quite true." the wiz admitted.

"And," Golter pushed, "if we didn't follow the Rules we wouldn't have light."

"True. But—"

"And to have a productive society we all must do our assigned duty." With that, Golter sat back down on the ground, once again folding his arms.

"Quite right!" the wiz softly agreed, grinning, as if this Common Servant Folk had fallen into a well-programmed trap. "So we have to get enough of the Folk to slave and work hard to keep the Lights lit. Keep them Social Wheels rollin', Folks, keep 'em rollin' along, otherwise the Walls might come tumblin' down. What would happen to our World of Walls...then?"

"Yes," Golter wanted to know, "what if us so-called common folk didn't blindly follow the Book of Rules?"

"Well, if that fires your engine...so...You have my permission to worship before Godwall's Book of R's. If you want or need my personal permission, which is, at the best, of very questionable authority, come to think of it."

The two men merely nodded in open agreement to that last statement.

"Well, in any case. I won't stand in your way."

"Nice of you," Golter retorted. "You truly are so generous."

"And. I ask, no, demand, the same from you. Be generous. I wave my arms in the air. Servant, you Serve. So do it" The words were biting, bitter, flaked with hard contempt. "You, Strong Man, be a mighty Warrior. Find and kill those silly little Dragons. Just let me wave my arms."

Mhyo felt a flush of annoyance at the young man's snide remarks. "You are nothing but words," he snapped in thoughtless contempt. "A wizard of no great matter or magic power."

"You want demon tricks to demonstrate power?"

Golter challenged with: "Yes, change something into something...well...else. Prove your Power of Wizardy."

"I should turn you into a snake? Make you something you aren't? Create stupid FXs to Razzle Dazzle foolish folks? Change you into a frog? Give you wisdom through tricks? Well, one can not make you what you aren't!"

"He's insulting." Golter remarked to Mhyo. "Are you going to sit there and let him insult us?"

Mhyo considered, said: "Surely you can offer more than insults."

The wizard considered Mhyo, then sighed. "Well, I could...let's see. Okay.!" The wiz lifted his arms into the air, continued: "Now watch with your mind, be willing to accept. Gaze into my eyes and really see—if you dare or can—through my senses."

Those arms slowly moved, making short circles.

Mhyo felt as if he'd been drawn into a monstrous black hole, deeply yanked through some time portal. A dark channel closed in around his total awareness, sucking away Reality. The black was followed by splashes of light, color. Red blinded him, yellow soothed, green caressed. The colors formed indefinable patterns. Then suddenly the world reappeared.

The wizard stood there, arched forward, arms swaying. The very atoms in the air flowed around him like rivers and waves, became swirling movements of fantastically colored stars. Galaxies gathered together, as if the universe were recreating itself. Space and Time buckled into raging colors; reds, oranges, blues, purples, greens, deep yellows, all splashing in on one another. Wave after wave of light surged up around wizard's body. Sound murmured softly to form a whispering music.

The undulating rainbow of colors and enchanting sound embraced Mhyo in an ecstatic crunch of pleasure. Could a woman's embrace ever be as sensual? All this radiated from the air around wizard's moving arms. The experience was almost over-whelming.

All at once Mhyo could actually feel the pres-sure of a phantom Princess body embraced against his own. It was like in the hundreds of Erotic Fanta-sies that plagued his night dreams. Then he experi-enced what seemed a very real surge of pleasure ram up through him. The eruption of a volcano could not have been more intense, nor violently heady. It shattered his frame like a lava flow. He convulsively shuddered, trembling in the aftermath.

Then, suddenly:

It all vanished. Instantly. As if sliced away by the bold stroke of a broadsword.

The wizard's arms had dropped to his sides.

"Have you seen?"

Golter shook his head. "Nothing."

Mhyo merely stared wide-eyed at the wizard, but said not a word. He was trembling. Where had such visions come from? It was like all his dreams slapped together into one Mighty Whamo! Could any Princess match this illusion?

"...I do my Art and it is something very beauti-ful to me." The wizard's words faded in and out. "...It is beautiful to me. And pure life. That is magic. Enjoy what you are....not caring what others think."

A moment of silence followed. The hard words commanded: "Go—leave me to experience myself to the fullest."

The wizard began once again waving his arms in the air, but now totally ignoring the two men.

Mhyo, without a glance back, mounted his horse, and hurriedly directly it past the young wiz-ard. He was completely unnerved.

Some time later Golter broke the long silence, "Why did you let that...that so-called wiz talk that way? You should have killed him."

"Your being foolish, my friend," Mhyo answered in a dreamy voice as he directly the horse down the path towards the valley below. He was tempted to reveal his experience under the wizard's spell. But didn't. "The man was no threat."

"He was insulting," Golter snapped back. "That's enough."

"Words, nothing more. Certainly he is really harming nobody. He believes his magic. Why mock that? Why cut him down? More important: he's no Dragon."

After a moment of consideration, Golter nodded. "I guess you are right. But he did anger me. Waving his arms and saying such silly—No magic there. Even if he did that finger...gag. That's hardly magic.."

"He did know our names."

"Maybe we're already famous?"

"Hardly."

They had reached the bottom of the cliff, and here is where the road forked three ways. And no signs posted.

"Which one?" Golter wanted to know.

"All roads lead to Deathwall," Mhyo reminded them.

"Some are shorter than others," was the uncertain retort. "I, personally, am in no hurry..."

"But I am!"

Golter pondered the roads. "Left, right or middle?"

"This way!" Mhyo decided. "Right down the middle!"

The Warrior's horse broke into a swift run, enveloping Golter in dust. The servant sighed, and faithfully followed, wondering what their next encounter with the unknown would reveal? Dragons? Or more foolish voices? Perhaps Maidens of silken flesh? This last thought drove Golter eagerly forward. Maidens were to him what Dragons seemed to be to Mhyo. And thus they continued until darkness folded around the world.

MID-SECTION, THE CITY, AND MUCH MORE

[Editorial Note: The following section is based on incomplete fragments.* It hints at many diverse— and lost— adventures. Sadly very few details survived. These small sections were scattered over a great portion of the original, ancient document. Much was unreadable; what remains is frustrating, inviting, suggestive. Most of all we are left with hints, quick snapshots, short "videos" that taunts the imagination. The editors have attempted, here, to piece together the few, most important portions. In some cases there was nothing but the name of some exotic locale to indicate what might have been a grand, though lost, adventure. Their visit to the City appeared to have been a major event, though very little has survived—one can only wonder about the missing parts. Some of the other places they went to are merely noted, reconstructed from half sentences.

*Brackets, [...], are used to either indicate short (within paragraphs and sentences) and long portions when isolated as a paragraph.]

.

The Drags of Dressor

In the following days their activities ran the normal Gambit of Events necessary to qualify as a prime example of the standard Warrior's First Adventure through the Lands of Speaking Walls. The journey was constructed to test Mhyo's newly honed Warrior Skills.

At one point [they] walked through the famous Markets of Wilding, sampling local native treats and [...] a few days later visited the ancient Torno Cliff dwellings, followed by the standard tour of the Ruins of Leints. All this came as part of Mhyo's pre-packaged Travel Kit. Riding the Rapids of Tartartarian, down the Zeloto River, proved exciting, but hardly more than a [nice] diversion.

[...]

[At the roadside] newsstand, the [seedy] man leaned across the wooden counter, and cried out at them. "Wanna buy a map?"

They merely glanced his way. [Then he] yelled: "I know where the Dragons are!"

That stopped Mhyo. He turned and stared at the shabby, isolated shack plunked down next to the jungle [road].

"Yeah, Warrior, I know how difficult it can be. Lookin', searchin'. Tryin' to discover where them Drags are hidin' themselves. Well, do I have a Map for you! Believe me. I have the best...est, must detailed, great...est and...well, never mind that. I have just what you're need to cap a Drag or two..."

The gnarled hand lifted out from under the counter, holding a thin pamphlet. "Direct from the...well...whatever they call it. Publisher. Yes. The Publisher of World Maps, Inc. This is from their SubSid, which releases special editions just for the standard touring Warrior...and his servant, of course. You've lucked in. This is a News Flash. Never before seen by man nor beasts. This is right off my private, newly installed, PC! Says so, right here...new discovery of the...er..." The man glanced at the pamphlet. "Oh, yeah, the Drags Home Base. They call it Dressor! Hey, that sounds pretty promisin', don't it?"

Golter shook his head, muttered out of the side of his mouth: "Sounds like a cheap huckster to me."

Mhyo wasn't listening. His attention was totally jailed by the pamphlet. He dismounted. "Home Base?"

"You know, where they live, where they go at night, where you can find them...they're supposed to be all over the place."

"Nothing I have read said anything about a Home Base—"

The man leaned forward, winked. "Secret. A brand new, just discovered, very secret place. Nobody knew about it...until...well...yesterday, maybe last week. Well, when ever the story says they discovered it. I told you, this is a Special Edition, hot email off the local PC...BBS...or ONLINE...what ever they call it...News Service.. You'll have a jump on all the other Warriors...and servants." Those eyes

70

glanced at Golter, then returned to Mhyo. "Just a buck a pamp."

"Buck a pamp?"

"Buck, coin, or wherever you have of value. What do'ya think?"

Golter, now standing next to Mhyo, simply stated: "I think we should go. Now!"

Mhyo was fumbling in his Warrior's pouch. He had some change there somewhere. Finally he discovered a small, flat coin, which he timidly offered the man. "Is this good enough?"

"I suppose. If that's the best you can do. A buckaroo. Come to think of it, not bad. Pretty hard to find, them buckaroos, that is. Where'd you get that?

"Back there [...] [The waitress] in the local tav gave us change."

[...]

Much to Golter's verbal shock there actually was a Dressor Valley, though hardly anything like [they might have] expected. No lush jungle, no meadows. It was a place with plenty of stones and desert sands, hills and valleys stretching off in all directions. The map claimed that Dressor was a prime location for Dragon Hunts. Even the newly erected sign outside the entrance claimed that:

Dressor is for Drags.

In three long, hot, days, they had discovered nothing more exciting than a lizard and several cockroaches. After more days of such fruitless search for Drags in Dressor, both men were just about fed up, tired and discouraged. Golter, though, was far from sad about the lack of even little creeping crawlies with sharp teeth. He, quite frankly, my dear, didn't give a damn about coming face to face with any monstrous Dressor Drag. He simply wanted to get on with their travels and out of this barren valley. The short of it was: it was Time to Go!

This was one of the few times when their life-long friendship almost frayed to the point of shred-ding apart.

By the morning of the seventh day, Golter was quite finished—the end, no more rocks, no more stones, no more Dressor sand. Kaput. Ende. Good-bye, see ya ol' bud. Let's get outta here. Both men's [temper] had been chopped raw to the [shatter-point]. Even before they left camp they started argu-ing.

"Why not accept the fact that you won't find any Drags."

"You're just being negative. Quitters never Win."

"I'm realistic. Suckers...well...just suck."

"You're a downer."

"At least I'm no all-day sucker."

Ignoring that, Mhyo stated: "And downers are dull. Just no fun."

"What does fun have to do with Drags?

"I think they'd be grand sport."

"You would," Golter observed, almost unemo-tionally. At least Dragons weren't Deathwall. "But there ain't no Drags in Dressor. And that's not being a downer—either! I'm simply being realistic. And I resent you calling me a downer."

"Well you are! And that's final!" Mhyo lead the way across the rocky plain.

Two days later they picked up the argument as if it had never stopped. Right after leaving camp Mhyo stated: "Please, today, try being not so negative. I don't need any more Negs. I need your support. I need to hear uplifting strokes. I simply can't take any more defeatist remarks. Pick up your attitude. Give me a Positive Grin. Keep those Good Thoughts radiating out of your mind and encouraging me on. It isn't fun being the only positive person around on such a terribly hot, disgustingly miserable day. So I want nice, soothing, cool-headed, [positive thinking] words from you to [sooth] any discouraging [thoughts away]. Simply put: I what you as an upper."

"Downer or upper...name don't change a thing." Golter muttered half to himself. "I see the truth...quite clearly."

"You don't see at all."

"I see what is around me. No dragons. Big or small."

"Positive. Just PosThoughts. Be supportive."

"I won't promise. Even the Snake didn't promise—"

"Forget the snake, damn it!" Mhyo snapped, slapping sweat from his eyes. "God of all Walls, its hot."

"Tell me something new," Golter complained. The other ignored the remark.

Much later in the day, after Mhyo had looked behind, around, and under all sorts of boulders, the two broke for the afternoon meal.

Mhyo, watching Golter eat, complained: "You sure gobble the food for somebody who sits by while I yank and pull boulders."

Golter was hungrily finishing off a third BLT.

The Warrior continued: "You haven't done anything more than sit on your horse, watching me do all the work."

"You're the hunter," Golter pointed out, wiping his lips.

"Your the servant. I'm the master. You serve. I master."

"Then master if you must!"

"It's about time you helped. You haven't picked up one rock. Not one stone. Not one boulder. Its your turn."

Golter shrugged. "I'm here to serve."

"So serve. Pick up that rock over there." Mhyo demanded, pointing.

Shrugging, Golter stood, moved to a rather big rock, easily lifted it up over his shoulders, high above his head. Nothing was there except a small black insect. In disgust, without thought, Golter dropped the boulder on its tiny back. "So there. You filthy creep!"

"What are you doing?" Mhyo frowned in surprise.

"Killing the only dragon in this empty place. There aren't no Drags here! Even you can see that."

"I see—"

"Rocks, sand and nothing." Golter stood there, furious, hands on hips, glaring at the desert. "If you want to look any further you can do it yourself! I'm quite finished with Dressor."

Mhyo stared at man, seeing the furious anger in those broadly spaced eyes. "After just one stone? You quit after one stone?"

"We've been here for too many days of stone picking! If you're so positive, so Up...purred...so Pos-i-Tiv you'll find the required number...why not...not...well...you ...you can do it alone...."

The man mounted his horse, then turned, faced Mhyo. Dramatically extending his arm, pointing blindly, not even bothering to look, he challenged: "Why not pick up that rock over there? Surely you'll find one of your fab Drags under it! Or take that one, over there. Or...that one. If fact, pick up any rock!"

Golter continued to point with a trembling hand. The anger swelled in uncontrolled fury. "There aren't no Drags in this...place!"

"You have no faith," was Mhyo's reply.

"So call me a non-believer, if you must."

"I gotta find at least one Dragon." Mhyo sounded desperate even in his own ears.

"You're obsessed. You talk about uppers and downers and I wonder...what was in that map. You act like you've been drugged."

"You know all Warriors are Drug Free."

"Yeah, yeah. Drug Free and all that. But not sucker-free. That newsman knew when he saw an all-day Dragon Sucker."

"A...what?" Mhyo was quite discouraged. "A Dragon Sucker. What's that?

"A Dragon Sucker. A Dragon Sucker. You know, the dummy who'll buy a fake drag map. An innocent, stupid, dragon-hungry Warrior-type. He had your number. All the way to the Nth degree, and then some. He saw you were obsessed with Dragons. And that sucks!"

"What?" Mhyo screamed, standing, hand touching the sword at his hip. "What're you saying?"

Golter sat there on the horse, breathing hard, face beat red.

"Well?" Mhyo challenged., fingers gripping the hilt.

Golter said nothing, but face turned hard, grim.

"Well?" Mhyo demanded, starting to pull the sword out of its sheath.

Golter's eyes fixed onto the half-drawn sword, the afternoon sun flashing off its gleaming blade. His voice actually shook, saying: "You would kill me?"

They had been friends too long. "You would kill me? Your best friend. Your lifelong buddy. Your Pal. Travel companion. Servant. And all that. You would kill me? I can't believe what I'm seeing."

Mhyo didn't move. Sweat was dripping down his forehead, into his eyes.

"This is the act of a loyal, pure and magnificent Mighty Warrior? The proud seeker of truth. What would the Princess think of you now?"

Things were totally out of control.

That last sank in. With a sigh, Mhyo released the blade. It clanked back into place. He threw up his arms. "Maybe you are right."

"You bet I am."

"But I got to find my required amount of...Dragons—Don't I?"

Muttering to himself, Golter said: "He's obsessed. Truly obsessed."

Then very loud, he announced: "Time to leave this place. Time to give it up. Time to go. There aren't no Drags in Dressor—"

MORE PROMISING PROMOS

The advertisements concerning Tavern Maidens were everywhere, in every local pub, every wayside fast food stand. Even Family Motels had the standard Maiden Escort Flyer stuck in back of their guest books. Mhyo managed to ignore their blatant promises of strange interludes in romantic places.

Golter, quite naturally, was fascinated by the local papers, and their Personnel Section, generously cluttered with suggestive copy. [...] [So when they] stayed in a TravInn, both [men] enjoyed the local papers. While Golter [was] feasting on all graphic ads for Maiden Escort Services, with their promising pics of maidens willing to [...] and much more [...] Mhyo ardently devoured all Dragon stories—major or minor. Any lead might serve up a Dragon Kill. He actually bought a book titled: Secrets of Dragons. It promised to be a tell-all about their life style. It claimed to tell where they could be found! And it sure revealed a lot about their eating and hunting habits. One section, though, titled "Their Private Lives: SubSection: The Strange TriSexual Mating Call of the Terrible Rex" gave him some problems. He didn't consider himself a prude, but was uncomfortable reading about such intimate animal affairs. Mhyo had no interest in the sexual manners of any creature, big or small; human or otherwise. Then under the caption "Measurements and Stats" he discovered the down and dirty details concerning the various size of a Drag's [...] He was embarrassed by the very minute detail of these rather graphic reports. (The scientists were, of course, quite frank in recording every fact. How, in the Land of Walls, had they managed to set up the lab experiments?) And Mhyo was [down right] dedicated [about] forcing himself through all these [disturbing details]. Nothing of any real value surfaced from the Private Lives of Dragons. The rest the book offered mere legends and rumors, puff pieces and "fictional" accounts of strange encounters in the night—and day. Nothing more. The local Tabloids were even less helpful, through, of course, quite amusing. Their headlines banners read: "Drags From Outer Space Devour Maiden Wives" and "She gave birth to a half Drag on the Half-Shell, late at night in the Cave of Passion." The one Golter especially liked was: "Dragons in the Orgy House."

As they continued towards the center of the Land of Speaking Walls, the road signs became bigger and bolder. Then they came to their first really big Mod BillBoard and got quite a surprise. For it announced The City. All their lives they had heard about the Famous City located at the very Center of the Land of Speaking Walls.

The BillBoard stretched alongside the ever-widening road like the side of a huge building. The sign displayed a big painting of Steel and Cement SkyScrapper buildings. Above this, across the top was printed, in vivid yellow letters, the words:

Our Land's Most Modern Town!
THE CITY

The two men, as they stared at the sign, grew very excited, each for different reasons.

Mhyo decided, "There will be Dragons in the City."

"Sounds like a Grand Ol' Opray, if you ask me," Golter quipped.

"Well, if they aren't there, where else would you find them? I mean, the City is a perfect place to hide many a local Dragon Den"

"I read, the other day, in the NewNews that the CityCops had Netted a Raid on such places. Shut down the Dens."

"They'll be Dragons. Surely. I truly believe."

"That you do. A Real Believer. Just don't send no checks to the local Minister of the True Faith Church or—

Mhyo laughed at that. "Hardly. I just believe in Godwall and in—

"Yes, that you do. Thank the Walls that Speak."

"Wonder what else we'll find in the City...."

"Lotta great stuff. That's mod civilization. We might find delicious foods. Beautiful women. Exciting entertainment. Willing maiden Stage shows. With ToplessGirls. Yes. Women Maidens ga-loRe he he ...us."

Golter eyed a smaller poster stuck to the Bill-Board.

"Maidens for sale. Passion Street offers it all."

He pointed, said: "Now that's my kind of street."

"That's all you think of, isn't it?"

"Maiden are more fun—and safer—than Drag-ons. I'm just not all that thrilled about facing a man-eating monster Drag, even with you at my side to do the nasty...killing." Golter grinned. "I'd rather have a warm bod to share my bed."

"Do what you like!" Mhyo retorted, far more angrily then he had meant to sound. "Do your...carnal...best, if you must. Just don't involve me! I have the picture of my Princess to keep me warm."

"Some pic. Some warmth!" Golter observed with sad amusement.

"In the locket next to my heart," Mhyo assured him, patting his chest.

"Well I'm makin' the maiden dens."

"Well, you are a grand maker of maidens."

"You mock me, dear friend," Golter muttered, uncertain.

"I don't and won't mock you," Mhyo promised. "Just keep it to yourself."

"Geeze, thank you, oh mighty Daddio!" Golter exclaimed, still grinning.

"And I'll find my Dragons!"

"You and your bloody Drags. Sure. Kill Kill Kill!" Golter studied another road sigh that prom-ised the unlimited pleasures of Passion Street.

Mhyo continued to proclaim: "My blade will drain their wicked blood-bloated hearts. And I'll kill them. Dead."

"Dead. Kill them dead," the servant repeated in the required, loyal chant-like voice.

"I'll kill them dead," came the agreeable reply.

"You'll kill them totally and completely dead. Sure, sure." But the man's eyes had already found yet another sign to savor; another vision of a lovely maiden, just pleading to be...made.

Mhyo's steel eyes narrowed, the muscles of his body flexed tight, determined. He pointedly ignored those flyers. More or less. Gulping, he once more bragged: "I will surely kill many Dragons in the City!"

FIRST NIGHT IN THE CITY

"PASSION STREET"

The two men road to the top of the mountain and looked over at the deep, expansive valley below. They had expected a huge place, but nothing this [large]. The main section of the City took most of a Great Green Valley, surrounded by hundreds of Commercial Farms and—
[...]
What had appeared, from the mountain top, to be just a white line crossing the valley floor turned out to be a huge concrete road, upon which the [traffic] of the multitudes massed together [to enter] and exit the City.
[...]
It was in [this manner], crushed in the [mass] of Folk, Country and Suburban, that they entered the maze of steel buildings and plastic jungle streets.
[...]
[They stabled] their horses, then took a room at a Center City TravInn [...] [After dinner] Golter suggested a look around the immediately area. And around they looked! The man was quite anxious, and [seemed to have] some destination [in mind].
[It was] not long [before he] cried: "Here. This way."

Mhyo was all but shoved into a large walkway. [The building] they faced was huge, its arched entrance revealed a massive [lobby...]. A bright red neon sign announced:

HOLY TEMPLE OF THE SEVEN

Don't miss:

THE CHORUS OF THE VIRGINS!

Mhyo, with some surprise, realized this was the famous MotherTemple of the notorious Order of the New Creation, as Revealed by the Divine Seven. A somewhat successful Pop Goddess Cult. The Godwall Conservative Movement had been trying to close their traveling revival shows, but with little success.

"Not in there?" Mhyo objected, alarmed.

The appeal of this Order to women in the Land of Speaking Walls was rapidly growing at alarming rates. In actual fact the latest PopPoll ratings suggested the cult would effect the outcome of the next Lands election.

Mhyo continued with: "That's not a place for real men!"

Golter shook his head: "No. Never. Though...that Chorus of the Virgins...sounds almost inviting. But no. No fanatic Maids for me. None of the equal-or-better crap. What I want is over there. Across the street. Let's hurry."

Mhyo shrugged, almost submissively. No respectable warrior would willingly embrace the teaching of the Goddess' Seven. Even if there had been many male converts to its teachings. He wondered why.

[The street] into which Golter fairly pushed Mhyo was [thickly packed] filled with [people].

It took Mhyo only a [few moments] to note that the many women were scantily clad, the outlines of their lovely bodies [boldly displayed] under the flowing gowns [they wore].

Mhyo's eyes now [...] [were] unable to [see] ... all the details, the sights, the undulating tangle of [men and women]. Some [were] coupled off [...] locked in strangely contorted [positions].

Before he could fully analyze or respond to these [lusty] sights, he felt warm fingers caress along his arm. This created an automatic wave of pleasure.

"Oh, my, you are surely hard, you are!" a throaty, highly seductive voice murmured in his ear. "Hard as rock." Squeeze went the fingers. " Rock hard." Squeeze, squeeze. "Iron rock-hard." And another double squeeze. "Iron-rock steel-hard" Followed by a very long, slow but firm caressing squeeze that ran the length of his arm "I love it!"

Mhyo turned to look down at a woman standing right next to him. Her thick short fingers were grossly pawing the bulging muscles of his arm. The pock-marked, repulsively vulgar face was disgustingly coarse and fat, the eyes cold gray, the lips overly thick red smears. She must be at last 45! Both in age and in chest measurements. But the throaty voice was all hot, professional, passionate promise. "Are you that firm all over?"

"No!' Mhyo cried, trying to tell her to get away.

"I don't believe it." The woman's eyes lowered. "You are surely a man of stone. A hard man needs a soft woman." She wiggled, so that the huge fat bosoms plopped against the loose cloth of her dirty blouse. "I can give you such pleasures that—"

"No!" he muttered, forcing her clutching fingers away from his arm.

"What's wrong, luv? Don't you like women?" She shrugged [...] then disappeared into the crowd.

Two, far more attractive, much younger females took her place. One was bright blonde, the other with hair dark as night. Just beyond them he saw Golter embracing a voluptuous redhead, hands playing against the woman's [...] Three other maids pressed eagerly close to him.

"She's a pig!" a soft, lilting voice announced, drawing his attention away from the servant. "But we can offer any sport a sporting man like you could possibly desire."

Mhyo gulped hard as he saw how the two young women's bodies almost touched his. It was the blonde who spoke. "Norha's a fat gutter-slut. But we...are a big cut above that. We're the Dark and Light Duo."

Looking at the blonde, he said: "I supposed...you're—"

"Light. She's Dark." Fingers gently teased the flesh of his arm. Tingling pleasure followed her touch.

The dark-haired girl licked full lips. "We're better than these other trickies. We're famous City Wide." As she spoke, her hand slid across his wide chest. "You're surely some muscle to look at. We'll give you a double at a fair price."

"A double...what?"

"You know," the other girl winked, her hand caressed his chest. "Real pleasure, like you've never known. We're a great team. Ask anybody. We're the Double Duo. The best duo on Passion Street."

Mhyo stood there, momentarily helpless, experiencing the teasing, wicked pleasure of their seductively soft hands on [him].

The blonde, who called herself Light, surged closer, whispered, "I'll service you real cheap...the first Time Around."

Dark add, "Special rates for Virgin Tricks."

"What are you talking about?" Mhyo objected, suddenly very embarrassed. "What makes you think I'm a...a...well...?"

The two giggled.

"Only a Virgin Trick would be so shy and hesitant." Dark caressed his ear with soft, moist lips. "It's written all over your face."

"Well...well...I'm not a fool!" He gulped hard.

"Who said you were? You're just one of those loyal, young, fresh-out-of-school Warrior- types, determined to find dragons to kill in order to win their princess. Does that just about uncover it?" they both seemed to asked.

"How'd you know?" Mhyo had the overwhelming desire to grab this Duo into his arms. He really wanted to fully ravish their deliciously curving bods. After all, he was a strong, young Warrior in his prime.

Light's lips were soft and moist as they brushed his cheek. "I'll service you so well you won't want me to stop—ever!"

Dark promised: "Then I'll do it until you hurt, all over. Every. Where!"

"Service me? You think I am a machine?"

"Hon," Light laughed, fingers gliding down across the muscular knots of his stomach, "we have no illusions about that. For sure. Even if you feel so hard hot you'd melt rock soft. In fact, in our profession we have no illusions at all! Especially about Warriors, Virgin or not."

"Profession?" He knew exactly what they were. But he needed to buy time—his, not theirs.

They now almost sang in unison: "We're your Top Flight Super Pros. The bang-up Twins for lonely Joes."

Then Dark promised:" We'll fan your fires."

Light added: "We'll smother your bod."

Then, speaking in unison [they] concluded: "So just submit. We're hot! Real-lay Hot. We're Super Pros. With X-ta-Cee. We're Double Plus. Just take our Key? Submit. Submit!"

"No. I can't. Never!" Mhyo protested. He had to get away from them. Before he did Submit-submit. "My Princess would—"

"Not know a thing!" they assured him. "What's with you Warrior-types?"

"Nothing!" Mhyo assured them. "I'm just loyal and—

"Pure...for your Princess?" Light offered in a matter-of-fact voice.

Dark complained: "Just like all his type. Until they learn the truth."

Light asked: "You want to be a bumbling Virgin on your wedding night?"

"A fool," Dark offered, seductively winking, "that doesn't know when?"

"Or where?" added Light, with a bright twinkle in her lovely blue eyes.

They both giggled, then together said: "We know when. And we know where.

"Most of all, we know how."

Dark's hips ground voluptuously. "How and—wow!"

"We dish out the hottest tricks & treats. We burn your flanks. We'll cook your—"

Dark raised her hand, silencing Light. "I know just want he needs."

All innocence, Light asked, with a toss of her blonde head. "What does he need?"

"Oh, you know what he needs. A little of this and a little of that." Dark's hand boldly tapped the [unmentionable] parts of her body.

Light sighed, in what seemed like real pleasure. "Just think of it, Warrior. To know the such pleasurable treasures? Why she's offering her famous trio delights. And bet you can't imagine what I'll reveal to your [...]."

Shaken, Mhyo just stood there, fascinated by the wanton display.

"Well?" Dark asked. "What do you think?

They waited a moment. Then Light rolled her eyes, almost desperate, then said: "Maybe he wants a sampling."

Dark slid boldly against him. "All young Warriors come here to get their first experience, hon. And we're the best teachers in the town. Just ask."

"Ask...what?" Mhyo gulped, aware that her hand clawed boldly for what no princess-like woman would dare to seek. Well, not so publicly, anyway.

Mhyo's hand trembled as he pushed her [groping fingers] away.

"Oh, okay then!" Light sound resigned.. "You really swing a tough deal. So just for you, we'll give a free Run Around the Land. One time only."

The duo gazed across at him, now all cool business.

"Well?" they demanded.

Mhyo was stunned by the swelling sensations enveloping him. It was difficult to even think.

"Well?"

"No...go away..." His right hand clutched the locket that contained the picture of the Princess. He moved back, beyond their reach. Turned. Then pushed past the few women who attempted to block any exit from the narrow confines of [...] blindly crossing the street, he ran up the steps of the huge building —

[...]

The gigantic figures of the Seven Goddesses of Creation loomed along the walls of the domed lobby.

This [was the] Temple of the Seven Goddesses.

Mhyo turned, bumped into a very lovely young lady.

"Oh, watch out, Warrior." Those eyes glazed with deep interest as they met his.

"Sorry." Her slim body was quite attractive in the yellow toga that hugged it so gently.

"Oh, that's okay, Warrior." Her voice was now very musical, lilting, quite innocently pure. "I'm certain you didn't mean it."

When Mhyo tried to get past her, a gentle hand extended, touching his chest.

"Wait. Don't leave. I see you are a very confused soul."

"Confused?" That stopped Mhyo. He had wanted to get out of the building, return to the TravInn. "Confused?"

"Yes. But there is no need for confusion. You are pure at heart. You are surely a loyal Warrior on his first Grand and Holy Mission."

"Well...I..."

"Don't stammer. Don't be afraid. You are safe here. They can't get you here."

"They? Who?" Alarmed, Mhyo look around. What was she talking about?

"I saw how you ran from those horrible creatures across the street. They sell their bods for bucks. I don't blame you at all. We are dif here. We don't believe in their kind of gross, disgusting, perverse, unGodly carnal sinning. Horrible how they sell bods for bucks. We are pure, in the Temple. We Know only about the Divine Creation, the only True Love Power. We don't sell ourselves to any male beast that simply wants a vessel for [???]. We teach the only True Grand Morality. We give Truth, the Cap T, and [...] We Promise the Pure of Heart a Perfect Haven. Here all are equal. Beggar, Warrior, Woman, Thief. Street cleaner or maiden most pure. We all share the same Divine Perfection. Here you will Truly be safe. No wicked, sinful groping for parts too private to mention. You'll find no shame-filled offers from carnal perverts. Not here. This is the Haven of the Goddess' Seven. We are of the Divine Creation, the Truth Seekers in the Land of—"

"Okay. Okay, already," Mhyo cried, just exhausted. "Just let me out of here."

"Yes, I see. Of course. You need peace. You need the soft understanding that only the Seven can truly offer. You want the Pure, the Quiet, the Truth." She took his hand in hers. "Let me show you The Way."

[...]

The young girl led him into the huge chamber. She sat next to him, holding his hand in hers, as they listened to the invisible Speakers of the TempWall.

"We are the Tellers, We Reveal Creation. We Speak of the Seven Days [...] [And] She said, Let the fires swarm over the Hills and Valleys of the Lands. [...] And Mother Four Promised the Flesh of many Beasts to feed the People of the Lands. And Mother Five [...] fed you of the Creatures small and large."

With a [groan] Mhyo [struggled to be free of] the young woman's hands.

"Well," her words soothed, reasonably, "not everybody blindly accepts...at first, I understand." [She] clutched his fingers, directing [him] through another door, into an even bigger room. " I'm certain you'll enjoy the musical."

"The what?" Mhyo was dazed by too much input.

She looked up at him, eyes bright, pure and innocent. "Why of course. The Show!"

"What show?" All Mhyo wanted to do was leave.

"The Chorus of the Virgins, of course. I'm in it on weekends."

"Then you're a...show...girl?"

"Well, not the kind of show-all girl that sells her bod for bucks on Passion Street. None of that kind of stuff goes on here. We want to close down that evil place across the street. We're nothing like them. Our show is pure. Believe me. You'll like it, Warrior. You can't leave the City without seeing our Grand Off-Broadstreet Musical."

Dumbly, Mhyo let the young Temp Virgin take him into a huge theater.

The place was, of course, packed. On stage were women dressed in respectable togas, even if cut very very short to reveal lovely, long legs. The blare of music came from the walls, left and right. Then the girls, arms locked together, legs kicking high, started singing:

"We're the Chorus of the Virgin Temps. Virgin Temps. Virgin Temps. We're the Chorus of the Virgin Temps. Hooray, Hooray for us!

"We are the Chorus of the Virgin Temps, the Virgin Temps, the Virgin Temps. We are the Chorus of the Virgin Temps, Don't you think were cute?"

The girl's fingers squeezed Mhyo's hand. "Isn't this great? Aren't you having fun?"

She grinned so cheerfully, so happily up into his face that Mhyo found it difficult to do more than shrug. But during the [next half hour?] while the Chorus Virgins continued to kick and sing out their cheery routine, over and over and over again, without so much as a beat out of place, not one word, not one kick varied even a fraction, Mhyo wanted to yell: "Enough! Enough!" He was now quite sick of their Virgin pitch and kick. Even if their legs were Divinely beautiful. Instead, when the girl squeezed his hand once again, saying: "They sure are talented, aren't they?" he merely, very politely asked: "Do they know any other songs?"

"Oh, come on, Mhyo, of course they don't. If they did it would be another kind of Chorus, wouldn't it?"

"Oh," She was probably right, since titles defined. "I suppose so."

"They do it so perfectly, don't they?" she inquired, voice just flushed with brazen pride.

"I guess they worked hard to perfect their lines," he lamely offered.

"Yes, we all have to work very hard, each and every day, to get them down just right." Her words eagerly assured him. "We're really quite lucky to be a part of the show. A girl's gotta keep in perfect shape. See?" She lifted edge of her skirt, exposing a soft, smooth thigh. "I do have nice legs, don't I?"

He nodded. It was true. She had just perfect legs.

"Yes. It takes hard work and dedication to be a part of this show. You can believe me. Strong Faith, too. Only truly pure, hard working Virgins can dance the dance, sing the song."

The musical Chorus of Virgin Temps continued to chant and dance, quite without end.

A few more minutes and he said: "I think I got the point. Could we—"

"Natch, how thoughtless of me. It's time, anyway." She almost pushed him into the corridor. Neither spoke, though her tiny hand was soft and warm in his. As they came to the end of the corridor, she hesitated, turned to a door, said: "This is really your first date in the city, isn't it?"

"Date?"

"You know, me and you. Kinda like a date, don't you think. Our very first date." She took a key out of her toga, handed it to him. "Do you want to open the door for me, like a good gentleman should."

"Door?" Mhyo knew he sounded like the classic one-worded fool.

"My apartment. Please." Those eyes silently begged "Oh, come on, don't be shy. I'm a Temp Virgin. You have nothing to be afraid of from me."

He started to take the key.

"Believe me. I'm the most pure of all the Virgins."

He opened the door.

Taking his hand, she urged him into the room. "Come. We can do the Holy here."

"Holy?" Then he added, "The Holy what?"

The door slammed shut behind him.

"We are safe now," she announced. "Here, at last, alone together, in the privacy of my own rooms. How romantic. And...safe."

Safe? he wondered. From what?

As if guessing his thoughts, she quickly added: "Safe to do what the Divine Ones demand."

"Demand?"

She leaned against the door, boldly blocking any easy exit. "Of course. We're in my room. Now it is safe to kiss me. A sweet, pure, soft, first-date kiss."

"I haven't even kiss the Princess..."

"Oh, forget her. I'm here. She's there. And I'm a Virgin Temp. They expect me to do this at least once. Like they say in the Biz, the show must go on and on. And we Virgs must give the best show in town. Otherwise we'll be stuck in our lowly position forever. And that's a long time to be a Virgin Temp. So. You can kiss me." Her lips puckered, lifted, up close to his.

He didn't move.

"Come on, don't be shy. It is expected. We, of the Seven Goddess Temple, are as equal as any male, be they Warrior, Wizard or Godwall, Itself. And Wow, that's supposed to be really some trip. I mean, with the God of all Walls. Only the High Seven have managed to crash through that Ceiling..." She took his hand, placed it on her hip. "Come on, now, Warrior. Prove you are a True and Proud Dashing Prince of all Luvs. Plant it on me. Right here." She tapped her lips. "One goodnight kiss to seal the promise of our first date."

He just stood there, turned rigid [all over].

Just a bit anxious, she instructed: "Don't make me wait until I'm an old crone."

The warmth of her breath was heady. Just a kiss, he told himself. Just one little ol' kiss from a Virgin Temp couldn't be too harmful.

"It isn't as if I expect you to sweep me off my feet. I'd hardly, willingly, submit to being tossed on the bed, right there, just behind you, and forcefully ravished. Not on a first date, you can believe me, I don't expect that kind of knock-down, drag-it-out, hair-pulling, back-clawing, wild and wonder full-filling action. I just wouldn't expect that. Not from you, you darling, Prince of a Fellow, Dashing Male...oh, my, are you one fine hunk of man. I'd just wouldn't expect that from you. After all, you are a strong, powerful, Gentleman Warrior. You are pure and loyal. So, I ask but one kiss...to soothe the

95

burn of my lips. Just one, gentle, tender...first-date, of course, union of our...oh, don't keep me waiting another moment. Just kiss me. Once. Just like you wanted to give your Princess. Don't torture a woman like this. Don't make me beg. Don't make me fall to my knees before you in wanton passion, pleading. Please oh please."

Just one kiss was all he had wanted from the Princess, Mhyo reminded himself, trying hard to focus on the memory of her standing there in the garden.

"Just one. One. One kiss." Her words were almost hypnotic. "A kiss, a simple kiss. Just one is all I'll need."

But one kiss might surely lead to another, then another, and then another. Could he trust himself to be content with simply one kiss?

Even with a Princess?

Let alone with a Virgin Temp.

They were so totally, deliciously alone in her apartment. With the bed behind them! It was large and inviting. It offered such a haven for ravishing this so beautiful, so perfect, Divine, and, obviously, so passionate young Virgin Temp.

"Yes?" she murmured, "I am so very beautiful. Aren't I? So lovely. I am so Divine and lovely. I am so perfectly perfect for you. I am everything you could ever desire in a woman. Even if this is our first date. And I burn for your kiss. My bod trembles at the very thought of our lips blending together in a soft, warm, innocent, first-date, kiss."

"What's....this...date....stuff?" he stammered in a suddenly husky voice, breathing the words against her parted lips.

"First, last, mid. What dif? A date's a date. The label defines. Kiss me so I'll never forget you!" The words were actually moving those soft, hot lips against his. "Kiss me...all over! You dumb beast!"

That struck home. He whole body curled into action. Well, to be truthful, Mhyo never knew exactly what did happen. At one point in Time he was standing close to her, their lips just touching.

Then, as if jump-cut, he was trembling outside the Temple, panting, hard.

Dazed by the events of the past hour, Mhyo staggered as he moved along the walkway. He had no sense of direction, and never knew how he got back to the TravInn. The next clear memory was of stepping into the room. Golter, of course, wasn't there..

This first night in the City [had been] just too much.. The girls here were almost as dangerous as the dreaded Dragons . Perhaps just as dangerous. Perhaps, perhaps, perhaps. Maybe more dangerous. In their way.

Much later, when Golter returned, neither man said a word to one another. They knew it was best to leave the subject of Passion Street totally and completely off-limits. And Mhyo was not about to say one word concerning the lovely, delightful, delicious, Virgin Temp.

He lay in bed, trying to forget it all, as if it had been a bad dream—deliciously tempting though she might have been. His mind chanted: Forget her. Forget her. Forget...

WHAT ACTUALLY HAPPENED NEXT

[Every evening] Golter eagerly sought a Maiden Den. The first few nights Mhyo stayed in their room and attempted to sleep, desperately focused on visions of the Princess. As to the Virgin Temp, his chanting to "Forget her; forget!" had seemed to work—for the most part. Finally, though, he gathered the courage to begin night-trips through the [streets], searching adventure [and] those illusive Drags.

[...]

[The City] itself, [...] was a magnet to draw all kinds of Folk to its [heart?] . It was this mix that brought detailed texture to dazzle his still young and innocent [mind]. The Multitudes flocked from all areas of the Land of Walls that Speak—and, of course, they spoke the same tongue, even if with different dialectics. It was a matter of slang, and such, that marked the difference between suburban and rural Folk. Still, in most ways, the People of the Lands were of a single mind, even if differing in convictions and outlooks—amazing, considering the many varied Time-frames! While Wizards and Witches did their magic in the countryside, Scientists lectured in City Colleges; and Politic-minded Reps debated in the Magnificent Civic Halls. The Mighty Rich and well-off MidClass, and all other

98

such greedy holders of Stocks and Business Inks, haunted the Route of Gold Bricked Walls.

[...]

There were the ugly [Industrial Parks] and the more [crummy] gang invested ghettos, where poorer Folk survived—barely. These seedy, sad places might seem to contain dragons of sorts. The local Hoods were cluttered with [shacks] selling cheap magic and dangerous chemicals mixes offered as quick, momentary escape from desperate nightmare lives. ...[he] considered all this simply too sordid and depressing to waste [any] Time [visiting].

[Mhyo] also ignored, with very real and dedi-cated resolve, the tempting Wicked Adult Dens and the many streets like Passion.

Broadstreet, though, boldly drew attention to the expensive productions of famous Hit Shows—new and revived. Mhyo considered seeing at least one of the flashy Musicals or Plays, even if the overwhelm-ingly heavy ticket price was a bit stiff—even for a Warrior. [In the end] he decided this was something to share with the Princess. She would like that. Plus: their combined income would more easily absorb the expensive entrance fee. So in the end he put such pleasures off for a different Once Up On A Timer.

Plus, there were other things of greater impor-tance to [do].

[...]

The City offered a vast mix of ethnic foods to temp all the Folk to exotic taverns. Both Mhyo and Golter eagerly devoured the delicious fried, sim-mered, baked and simply raw foods from distant places. This was their only true mutually shared adventure. Though of little import.

They each were too involved in their own private hunts.

[...]

Art Centers and Libraries offered much to take in. The latter was cluttered with many books, over large or under small, concerning Dragons of any form, real and imagined. There were even varied theories concerning the True Nature and Origins of Dragons. One startling volume, quite slim and discouragingly technical, was titled: "The Reality of Dragon Images as Projected within the Confines of the Scientific Mind: Detailed Reflections of the Theory of the Make Believe vs. Actual Dragon Forms as Outlined by the Scientific Board of the Psi Convention of Speaking Walls." In fact, even the local data covering the subject Dragon was simply too massive for his brain to compute, with or without the mysterious complexity of the modern City PCs. After a seventh visit, Mhyo simply avoided the place as just too much for a warrior-mind to devour. A person could spend Eternity just reading! A neat way of avoiding all direct action; but offering no promise of Dragon-kill scores—thus no earned Status; no Princess. He decided to keep the search more focused on physical action—as a truly fine Warrior would—and, if nothing else, Mhyo was certainly a magnificently Fine Warrior, fresh out of school, and in his Prime, at that!

[...] Mhyo was certain he'd discover many dangerous Dragons among the Multitudes in the City. Yet no Dragons attack from dark alleys, nor did they dived from tall building tops.

[...]

By the end of the [editor note: unknown number] week, he was quite discouraged. His searches had been, up to now, improvised and offered negative results. Even if all this had exposed him to the sites and sounds of this complex Center of the Land of Walls. So, on [the third day of the eleventh week]...[he] stepped out of City Hall, clutching a newly published street map of this [grand] City. [Mhyo] had decided to start a more organized, logical and planned-out, detailed and precise search of the City. He would find his Dragons. One way or another.

BLOODY BATTLE AND WITCHES' SPELL

[They had been] in the city for [a long time (?)] before the Incident of the Alley Witch took place. Both men were doing their own type of cruising. Golter always found a fared maiden. He knew where the hottest dens lay. This particular evening, as usual, after dinner, the two friends parted company. Mhyo always referred to the City map to organize each nightly search. The pattern was quite logical; it started from their hotel room and circled outward-bound, each day expanding like a balloon. [The City] was a large, complex place of Mega Story buildings, some actually sunk as deeply underground as they lifted upwards into the sky. This night, though, he was wandering through the dark streets of Market Town, a popular shopping area during the day, but strangely empty at night. The shop fronts were gloomy, curtained, the doors barred.

Each block had its required alley, some actually half-hidden behind an arched front. But many of these alleys were dim places in which bums and beggars, street folk of questionable repute, managed to survive the night. Most of the alleys, though, were devoid of anything but garbage-filled barrels.

Some became the meeting places of crime sects or gang meets.
[...]
[The sound] of wind moaned through the buildings. [But he] was used to that murmuring [...] it was the scream that caught his attention. It came from an alley just a block away.

Mhyo's right hand found his sword, as he rushed forward. His eyes held to the distance alley.

Another scream of raging fury crashed through the night.

Then a brutal sounding voice cursed: "Hold her down. Hold the bitchie!"

The third screech was so high pitched that it hurt his ears. Mhyo had already reached the alley.

[The gang was] packed tightly against and around the screaming, kicking form. There were at least six [males] struggling to hold down what looked like a [female].

"Stop it, bitchie!" One brute kicked at the helpless victim, now half spread-eagled on the ground. Another of the [brutes] kicked, a third kicked.

"Stop fighting, bitchie! It won't help. Just make me real bad, you bitch."

A moan sounded, "I'm no bitch."

"Sure, you are. And ya pay. We'll fix you!" came the mean reply. "You're all bitches or witches."

"Don't let her spell you."

"She won't!"

"Just kill her."

"Fast."

"No, we gotta have some fun!"

"Yeah, real fun."

"Do her first!"

"Yeah, we gotta do her. Real good."

"Yeah, real good."

"Then kill her!"

At that point Mhyo leaped at [them]. [His] sword swung brutally in a search for blood.. Left, then right. The blade hardly hesitated as it cut through cloth, flesh and bone. Several bodies slumped silently to the ground. The gang didn't even realize what had struck them. His attack was too fast.

Blood splattered Mhyo's face as he threatened the two remaining brutes who were standing over the woman. It was only then that he noted how small their shadowy forms were. One of them lifted a hand, a strange weapon pointed at Mhyo's chest.

Without hesitation, his sword swung. A crackling sounded, and light exploded from the small weapon, splattered fire against the alley wall. The [now] one-armed figure slithered backwards, snakelike. Whimpering in anguish, he disappeared into the street. The last hooded figure, face pure white, merely backed away from the woman.

Mhyo made a fancy, complex movement with his sword, now dripping red in blood, slicing it through the air with a savage, whooshing sound.

The fellow ran in open terror.

[Mhyo's] eyes stared at the dead bodies. Stunned by what he saw. [...] They were [only boys], maybe ten or twelve.

"What's going on?" he asked, as the woman looked thankfully at him. "Are you all right?"

"I'm fine, Mhyo." Her voice caressed his name. She appeared to be very old, the face mapped with deep wrinkles. Her mouth was thin, barely hiding unevenly spaced yellowed teeth. "I'm fine. Now that you're here."

"What's this...all about? They're just kids."

"Kid...killers." She waved a gnarled hand in the air as if to finalize her words. "They rape and murder. Just for fun. And—"

Mhyo was a bit stunned by that. "For fun?"

"And Points. Don't forget them. They get Status. Big Status. The more kills, the more the rank and file become bigger rank and smaller file. They gain status depending on their [number of kills]."

"Sounds like Status gained by Warrior's Dragon kills," Mhyo muttered, a bit uneasily.

"Hardly so, Mhyo." She smiled up at him, and seemed not quite so old. Her mouth opened slightly to reveal evenly spaced, whitening teeth, then closed once more to form into what appeared to be fuller lips. Of course, that was illusion. "Street Gangs are just groups of kids surviving in the only way they know how. The City Cops do their best. But....too many rules about Child Rights. You now how Godwall is."

"Conservative," Mhyo assured her, wiping his blade on the coarse cloak of one of the dead boys.

"Yes, very conservative. Too much so, if you ask me."

A soft, delicately shaped hand reached out and touched his cheek. "You have saved my life. They caught me when I was Musing other Places, other Times. It can be difficult even for a good witch."

"I thought they called you bitch."

She grinned, those eyes sparking, almost caressing over his strong form. "Bitch...witch...they don't care...they don't even know the dif between a good one and a bad one."

"And what are you?" Mhyo wondered out loud, only vaguely aware of the strange metamorphosis taking place before his eyes.

"What do you imagine I am?" she murmured, face uplifted. Now her mouth truly seemed full, the lips flushed, half parted in open invitation. The woman looked startlingly young, all things considered. It had to be a trick of the dimly lit alley. Yet she had seemed so old, at first. "What do you want me to be?"

A momentary imagine of the Princess formed in his mind. Just as suddenly it seemed that her face started to reform itself into [...]

It was illusion, of course, Mhyo assured himself. This certainly wasn't his Princess. The face faded, the lips became fuller again, the eyes turned deep green, the hair changed to a dull brown.

"I can't do that to you, Mhyo." The woman sounded almost sad. "That would be too cruel. You must earn your Princess. You must win her fair and clean. You must face your destiny, as Godwall dictates."

"What are you...?." Mhyo was coming out of some daze, as if he'd been drugged by the very fury of the battle. He stared at the woman's face, still inches from his. The illusion of her changing features was dazzling, but surely illusion.

"I can be anyone else you wish me to be. A lovely maid, a mature Goddess, a street nymph or a royal...well, whatever...but not your Princess faire."

Her features kept shifting, changing, young, lovely, hair turning from red to brown to blonde.

106

The last image was that of a very young woman in her prime. She was now quite voluptuous, breasts brimming over the low cut evening gown clutching tightly to the curving lines of this deliciously full body. " I can be what you wish. Anything you most desire. What do you wish?"

Again the image of the Princess formed in his mind.

"No. That is the only thing I will not offer. She is your reward only after you have...well...done the required. But...oh I wish I could tell you. Oh, how I wish I could tell you." The woman drew back, this time the face that looked up at him was older, more maturely lined, though still very attractive.

"Tell me...what?"

"Oh, Mhyo, don't you truly know? Do I...we...any of us...have to tell you everything? Won't you ever learn to speak out?"

Something in her voice reminded him of the Princess. Something in the tone and quality. "What will it take to convince you? What must you be told to understand? When will you open your ears and mind to...Oh, sometimes you can be so dumb!'

"I'm listening. Just tell me what you want," he pleaded. It seemed as if these very lines had been exchanged with the Princess.

"If you can't guess the truth, Mhyo, I...I...just feel sorry for you."

"I don't read minds. What do you expect from me?" Mhyo pleaded, feeling totally confused. This was the kind of argument he'd had with the Princess.

"Help me to understand."

"Take a stab at it."

"I...can't. I just...well...I..." He stammered, helplessly. "I can't guess."

"Try. Just try." came to almost desperate reply.

"What do you want me to say?" He exploded.

"Can't you guess the truth?"

"What truth?"

"About us...about, I mean, you and the Princess. About life. About anything. Just ...about."

He stood there in frustrated silence, staring at the woman, not certain who she was, where they were, or what Time Zone he was in. Everything seemed unreal, vaguely like an illusion, a contorted dream.

"Oh, really, Mhyo! You're impossible. Sometimes you can be so...so...well...just so! Men. When will they learn how to really treat a woman of quality. When will they...oh, never mind that."

They were silent for a long while. The alley seemed very quite. The light seemed to dim slightly. He actually felt a bit dizzy.

Then, standing suddenly very close, she reached out and very tenderly touched his shoulder. "Just don't forget the Power of Process."

"The power of...what?" He was painfully aware of the sensual pleasure of her touch. And a bit confused by her swift shift of messages. Though that latter was typical of maiden fair and unfair.

"Yes. Godwall instructed you. He said...let me see...something like: You will learn much from the process, the journey from here to there! Oh, well...something kinda like that. I can't remember every little detail."

"Remember?" Mhyo retorted, truly puzzled. "You were never there."

"Details. Mere details. I know much more than you might guess, Mhyo."

For the first time he realized she'd been using his name. "How'd you—"

"Know your name? Yes, of course. A bit of a puzzle, that, I suppose. I could say it is written all over your face—"

"That's not true!"

"Of course not, silly. So I won't say it. Enough that I know. Enough to say that I know much more. More than I can tell you. Even if you did save my life." The face swiveled up, aging into deeply cut wrinkles, as she backed away. Suddenly the woman was once more very old. "How can I put it? Let me see. A reward for a brave deed. I my not be a Dragon hiding in some dark alley...nor were those silly, foolish kids dragons of ol'...though far more terrible than the phantom dragons you haven't found, as yet...." Her voice trailed off.

They sat there for a long time, crushed by silence.

Slowly a misty fog gathered into the alley, surged around him. It became thicker. Mhyo looked at the woman, but she now was very faraway, out of focus. All shapes and forms blurred. Alarmed, he blinked, rubbed his eyes. Then all at once his hands flowed to his sides. He could see nothing, yet a sense of well-being replaced all emotion. He felt very tired. Terribly tired. This nightly search for dragons was turning into a very tired bore. The City was becoming a choking trap.

Suddenly [he] wanted to leave [the City] and once more resume [the] journey to Deathwall.

109

"Yes, Mhyo, leave the City. Tomorrow. Leave. Seek Deathwall and learn how to become more than you are."

The words formed in his mind; very dreamlike.

Then soft lips whispered gently into his ear. "Remember that even Mighty Dragons, be they small or large, no matter what their shape, no matter how powerful their magic, will fall before their own reflected power."

Mhyo opened his eyes, turned to reply. But she was alone.

The long alley was empty of life. Nothing moved. He was alone. Mhyo knew it was useless to search for the woman, bitch, witch or maiden; whatever she might be.

Perhaps she was all illusion. Perhaps a nightmare dream.

Then he saw the four young bodies lying on the ground in their own blood.

If they were real, all the rest had to be real.

[A dizziness] blurred all [senses]. Darkness wrapped about his mind like the coils of a snake. He could hardly breath. Gasping for air, Mhyo clutched at the rope-like folds closing on his throat.

A voice whispered in the black: "Even Dragons will fall before their own reflected power."

Mhyo cried out, then his hands ripped the covers off his body.

"What the!" Eyes wide, Mhyo saw the room. "How'd I get here?"

He was in his bed at the TravInn. Had it all been a dream?

The air seemed to speak: "Mighty Dragons, small or large, fall before their own reflected power."

Now he knew just exactly how real it had all been.

NOW FOR A FEW SHORT CUTS

The very next day [they left] the City, both with their own memories. [The] Warrior felt great confusion; he had said nothing about the encounter with the young Kid Gang, or the strange alley witch. It had been a very unnerving experience. What had happened to her? What had those closing words meant?

[...]

[They had, for days,] fought their way through the nightmare Jungles of Mapola, and then trekked across the Sea of Desperation.

Daily, new challenges were bravely met as they struggled through the diverse and sometimes Terrible Territories between the Speaking Walls.

Daily, our hero warrior sought dragons, but found no fire-breathing type creatures with lizard tails and huge Terrible Rex jaws.

[...]

Mhyo hunted the Horrible Korkadain, [from which he sliced] a large, meaty hunk of flesh. This Golter prepared for the long journey [across] the hot, naked sands of The Deserts of Maylayo

[...] It was here that a band of desert raiders, bandits in yellow capes, chased them for many hours, until a small canyon offered the perfect battle stage. Here no more than three men face them at once,

...[They] fought for what seemed a very long time, [raider] bodies falling rapidly to the sands at their feet...At one point, towards the end, Golter slipped in the bloody waste of a dead body and was almost killed[...] [It ended] when [Mhyo's] sword flashed quick into the raider's throat, swung clean across another's chest and deeply bedded into last desert bandit.

[...]

[they] mingled with a pride of Dalii Beasts, but were ignored by the Terrible—

[...]

[Then] the winged flock of Kai-di Birds, with claws the size of a man's head, a beak that could cut through bone, had proved to be no real threat. [His] sword sliced brutally through the leathery flesh, which turned green with [its blood].

[...]

During all these adventures, across the complex lands, Mhyo performed no true Deeds of Value grand enough to log on his Score Chart. Sure: he had saved an alley-witch; avoided seduction by lovely maidens—thank the Gods, grand and small, for that!—and, of course, killed many horrible beasts. But no Dragons—hits or misses.

Not even the suggestion of a Terrible Rex had passed their way. No sky-scraping, three headed beasts offered true challenge to his warrior's blade. Thereby: no Dead Drags, no Status—no Princess. Nada.

And now Deathwall loomed ever closer, even if, as dictated by the Map of the Speaking Walls, they still had far to go.

A PROFOUNDLY WAVING MOUTH

It was many days of hot travel through the parched sands of the desert, and long weeks across naked mountains, before they once again discovered more friendly lands of green forests and even greener valleys. Then they came upon the standard baked-brick country signpost. It had been neatly re-surfaced with cheap green plastic, on which was written:

You are about to enter:

THE FOREST OF THE WISE

The two men hardly stopped to read the words. It was enough to simply get past the terrible Territories that were now behind them. They continued on, past the sign, up the hill and down the other side.

A newer sign met them several valleys later:

This is the Private Estates of
A Very Profound and Learned
Personage

A short while later they saw the neon message that flashed just above the trees:

Listen to the Wind of Wisdom.
Be impressed by Its Wondrous Words.

Prepare yourself!

Golter shrugged: "I'm prepared. My ears are so open they burn!"

Mhyo laughed in good humor: "Considering all things, big and little, I do believe we are about to be exposed to Great Wisdom, indeed!"

But they continued for several days without sign or sound of wisdom. Then one morning a bright wooden sign, announced:

YOU ARE ABOUT TO MEET THE MOUTH THAT SPEAKS

It was late the next evening before they came to the Valley of the Voice—so another Welcoming Sign proclaimed. The sky was darkening, the wind blowing through the huge, thickly interwoven trees that matted the valley floor.

First came the whimpering sound that turned into a moan as it worked through the forest.

The wind sighed, then swelled. The moan focused, as if tuning itself to a distant radio station. It was very much like a voice.

"Aaaaaaaa.....aaaaa...."

A voice that almost spoke words.

The expression on Golter's face was consumed by puzzled concern. "Did you hear that?"

Mhyo was mentally focused elsewhere and it took a moment before he responded. He had, with building frustration, been reviewing some of the more interesting highlights of their adventures.

Thus, for the first time, Mhyo heard the wind.

The moaning seemed to focus tightly into a loud "Ahhhhhhh..."

"Hear that?" Golter cried, an edge of fear just teasing the words.

"What? What is it?" Mhyo wondered, coming out of his deep thoughts.

"Ahhhh...Ahhh......Ahh......Ah.....A.." The wind seemed to speak. "Pro...foun...d..."

Now totally alert, Mhyo pulled his horse to a stop as they came to a turn in the path.

The windy voice was moaning louder now and in the clearing before them a strange swirling mist formed where empty air should be.

A voice sounded sharply from the mist.

"A profound statement is a simplicity..."

"Who is there?" Mhyo shouted. "Come out, expose yourself."

The mist cleared suddenly, as if angry arms had swept it away, revealing a huge mouth, lips waving around large yellowed teeth. A dim haze of golden light surrounded the image.

"Why it is..." Golter stammered, unable to finish the statement.

"Nothing but a mouth," Mhyo finished.

"Very pro...found!" the mouth shouted back at them. "I'm nothing but a mouth! What does that mean? What are you...a warrior, a servant? But I don't mock your existence. I don't add that 'nothing but' routine."

Strangely, there was no real anger to the mouth's words.

"But...where is the... rest of you?" Golter inquired.

"You see all there is."

"A mouth...?" Mhyo squinted, puzzled.

117

"A very profound statement!" the mouth countered. "A very profound statement, indeed. But...my lad, always remember that a profound statement is a simplicity complicated by small minds trying to impress even smaller ones. Never forget that."

"I'm not being profound. Just stating—"

"Never mind that. Just remember what I said. A profound statement, simple or complicated, is nothing more than Grand words created by self-impressed minds to convince others as to their great and profound wisdom. How impressive to say something that sounds very important, and yet means nothing and everything and thus becomes meaningless."

"I don't understand," Mhyo replied, honestly.

"I'm saying you must complicate simplicity to impress others."

"Why not be simple?" Golter wanted to know.

"Why say it simply when you can awe those around you on how important and learned you are by complicating the obvious?"

"But why complication? Isn't it easier to say things in a direct and simple manner?" Mhyo wanted to know.

"Complication, my lad, is the very center of all great minds, be they gods or wizards or wizards or fools. Or snakes. For if one were to put all the simplicity of all there is in one statement of truth, nobody would believe it. Like: $E=mc^2$. Or maybe even Tripled? Well, no matter that. So, to impress those around us we must, of course, make things complicated. Thereby everybody can sit and think about the complication in order to somehow understand the simplicity which escapes them in the convolu-

118

tions of words and symbols and statements of little moment."

"But that's being a farce: Fool. Unreal. Hardly honest."

"Maybe."

Golter offered: "It is using tricks, if you ask me."

"What's wrong with tricks? Illusions? We wave our mouth in the air, misdirect the attention of our audience, and we can do amazing things. Thus all will begin to think we are a great Wizard. Yet all we have really done is distract the audience's attention long enough to do our so-called trick."

"But it is not reality—it is just a trick."

"That's what it is all about, my lad. And thus, as you will see, small minds complicate simple matters with the masterly confusion of many profound words and statements. They wish to cover up the frightening fact that they had little or nothing to say. Or, perhaps, that they have a secret of pure truth which they are frightened to reveal. The listener, of course, will surely not know the difference, if the statement is made with enough profound sounding words. So, to impress all those around you it is necessary to surely be very profound. See, it is all very simple."

"I don't see," Golter admitted.

"Complicate a simple truth and nobody will understand you. They will think you are very deep and learned and very important. If you say the truth very directly all the Folk will rightfully consider you a fool. For surely you are a fool to reveal all you know in such a simple and direct manner."

Both men glanced at one another in helpless confusion.

"And thus, my lads, a simple fool can be just a fool while being the most wise of men. And a wise man can be a simple fool. It all depends on how you look at it. Or how you express it. Or—how you complicate a simplicity."

"You speak nothing but words," Golter accused.

"Words, yes. They color, distort and shape and reshape, all for effect and all to hide the fool that we are from all others. Seek fools. They are willing to be truly honest. If you seek wise men and great Wizards and Gods, they will wave their mouths with fancy profound words to complicate ideas of simplicity. Thus they will confuse the People of the Lands."

"But, then, being profound is being...nothing," Mhyo suggested.

"Being profound is sometimes being a God or a Lord or a King or a General. Being profound is sometimes being one who is considered a great Mind. Being profound is...come to think of it, is being nothing."

"But there must be such a thing as meaningful..."

"Meaningful and profound statements. Words. What is meaningful today is not necessarily meaningful tomorrow. What is meaningful in our Lands may not be meaningful in some other mythical land. Though surely there must be some meaningful and real, or unreal, mythical lands. I mean, what is reality but an illusion of the mind? It is very much like a myth or fancy story or fantasy. It is an illusion of consciousness, conjured up by the mind control of one's own thoughts."

"But," Mhyo pressed, "surely there is meaning-ful—"

"Meaningful? What to? To what? Who? When? Where? And what given Time Zone, my boy?"

"Then there is nothing at all that is meaningful and real." Golter ranted in open amazement. "And true and—"

"Oh, there are many meaningful and true and real things. Even dangerous ones. Though only a very mindless fool will be able to ignore such...terrifying things. Of course, that does not mean those dangers will not be just as destructive to the real fool as they are to the wise man and Wizards...and even Gods. And certainly such a man as yourself and this Warrior."

"That's very confusing," Golter complained.

"See?" the mouth cried out in delight. "I wave my lips and you are impressed."

"I didn't say I was impressed," Golter bravely replied.

"Nor did you say you were unimpressed."

"Just confused."

"And to be confused is to be impressed by my profound statements—"

"Then," Mhyo offered with a tired smile, "I guess that means you are very profound. For you sound very foolish."

"Ah, maybe you are right. For to be profound is to be a good fool of fools. Especially when one knows that a profound statement is nothing but a simplicity complicated to Impress another's mind as to the mighty wisdom and power and importance of the fool speaking to them and—"

Somehow all had circled back to the beginning and it was obvious that this conversation would continue to go in profound circles getting nowhere.

"I'm impressed enough," Mhyo snapped, motioning Golter to follow him. "Enough of you...speaking mouth."

"If that's the way you feel...then I'll just leave you to your very profound quest for the answer that Deathwall has for you."

A mist started forming around the huge waving mouth.

Mhyo hesitated, asked: "What do you know about Deathwall and our mission?"

"Much more than you would like to know. Less than I wish to know. Since you are not willing to talk any further, and reject the greatness of my profound statements, I will only offer you the following idea: Great Wizards, living in large castles on hills will, sometimes, offer spells and wisdom, or simply a chance to discover greater understanding of what the World of Walls is all about, and what Deathwall means, and what your mission..." The words faded. Then after a moment the lips finished with: "Well. Enough profound statements for foolish ears who don't respect the wisdom of a waving mouth."

The wind blew through the narrow valley and the mist folded around the mouth, then suddenly shipped it away, disappearing.

Golter grumbled under his breath, shuttered slightly.

"I wonder what it meant about a great wizard..." Mhyo muttered under his breath.

122

A distant wind answered: "Seek the Great Wizard on the high mountain before the valley of Deathwall!"

Both of them turned around. That had been the voice of the waving mouth, distantly fading.

No mist was visible behind them.

"Too many voices to suit me," Golter complained. "I don't think this mission is worth the effort. All we find are a lot of conflicting mouths, snakes and self-impressed wizards who offer nothing but confusion. I'd rather be back with Mara the maiden most fair...or...for that matter any maiden, even if her fare is not freely given. I'll embrace all the soft, loving arms of any merry maiden of the city streets...or even of a lowly country tavern. I don't care. Though the maiden back home is certainly most fair of all. I'm not picky. Just give me a full, robust—"

"Enough!"

"Well, I'll take a maiden any way, rather than face...Dragons or...Deathwall."

"I do believe you're afraid of Deathwall."

"Ya gotta be kidding. Of course I am. Damn right!"

"I'm shocked," Mhyo laughed, good-naturedly. "Really surprised?"

"Don't be...I'm just your normal, average, foolish little servant guy, assigned to a Grand and Mighty Warrior. I am here to serve—not be brave. That isn't part of my programming."

"I suppose you are right about that. Must be difficult being a low born, common, servant type," Mhyo offered in a gentle understanding voice—of sorts. He hardly wanted to sound unkind.

"It is difficult at times," the other replied. "It sure can be that." Then more brightly. "The nice part of my position is where it puts me with the fair sex. They want; I want. And I don't have to deal with issues about how to...kill Dragons or...deal with Walls called Death—"

"You're certainly aren't shy about confessing your fear."

"Of Deathwall?" Golter retorted in soft whisper. He knew that all Gods of any size had big ears; or, at the least, a complex web of interlacing bugging devises to spy on the People. "I most certainly am totally and completely, without a question or a doubt, simple or complicated, very much in fear of the very idea of being within...Its grasp! I have no urgent call, no muse of the mind, no passion for lusting after the Deathwall's secrets, dark and deadly. I embrace no doubts about my position in this most magnificent and safe Land of Speaking Walls. And that is to serve you, but avoid quick exposure to the Wall most Deadly of all. You better believe it. Deathwall is not on my A list of vacation spots. Aren't you frightened?"

"Maybe. But I must do as Godwall says."

"Why?" Golter wondered. "We've come across many creatures who do not listen to Godwall—and they continue to survive."

"I must do my duty."

"Oh yeah, sometimes I forget. You warriors war, don't you?"

"I must do my duty," Mhyo repeated.

"To impress your princess?" Golter moaned, disgusted. "You're a bore at times. If you ask me."

"I didn't ask."

"No, I guess you wouldn't! Certainly not a Servant. Now would you?"

"Well...you are the Servant. I'm the Master. Names define. You serve."

"Yeah, and I serve a mean dish, too." But from the lustful expression in the man's eyes he quite obvious was thinking of hot, passionate maidens—not food. "I do that." Golter blabbered. "A real mean, pepper hot, super charged, passionately throbbing..."

"Let's go!" Mhyo commanded, cutting those words short. "Deathwall is waiting."

"I doubt that. Anyway, it is still some [distance]: Thank all the Gods of all the Walls that Speak." Golter grew silent. His face turned a little grim as visions other than maidens took possession of thoughts.

Generously, Mhyo said: "Whenever you want, you can return to your Mara or all and any of the maidens. But I must continued—and learn how to become more than I am."

THE TEMPTATION OF MHYO

[Editorial note: The following section might be nothing more than a fancy piece of erotic fiction within a farce. Many experts believe this was conceived by some crude hack who inserted it into the Dialogs. More likely, though, this is simply what remains of more detailed massages that an ancient censor felt was unnecessarily graphic. Even the Ancients had their bigots!]

For months the cheap, flashing signs and tavern ads had announced the House of Nymphs.

Golter read the first sign out loud: "The House of Nymphs, devoted to the Fine Arts. Fully approved by the Wall Gods' Board of Adult Education. Goddess Nymphs trained to Teach Beginning and Advanced Classes. Remember: What's good for the Gods is good for You. Your pleasure is our greatest reward!"

He turned to Mhyo, who was trying hard not to listen. "Boy. This is my kind of place! Sure sounds great to me. And God approved, too!"

"That's an ad. You can't believe everything you read."

"What's there to believe?" Golter was very excited. "I heard about this well...school.... Actually the most famous and Purr-fect CatHouse Resort of the Gods."

"Really."

"Well, look at that over there," Golter cried, pointing to another sign, read:

"'We'll treat you like a God and you'll feel just like one! You'll learn all the Arts of Love.' That sounds like a grand fun."

"Forget it!"

But the next days offered more road signs.

GIRLS, GIRLS, GIRLS

Mhyo managed to ignore most of these pronouncements.

Then at a crossroads they faced a very huge BillBoard. It displayed pictures of topless ladies:

Only 3 More Days To
YOUR SCHOOL OF LOVE:
The Estates of the Goddess Nymphs!
All Dragon-Seeking Warriors
—And their servants—
Are Invited
FREE OF CHARGE
To learn the
Wondrous Joys of Young Nymphs of Pleasure.
These are Expert Instructors.
This is truly your
Last Chance Classy Pleasure Lodge
Before the Final Encounter with
Deathwall

Across the road was the cheap MaidenTav. Nailed to the office was a blackboard with a chalk-written message:

> Don't wait!
> Get IMMEDIATE service.
> Mr. & Mrs. Smith,
> Warrior or not,
> Welcomed.
> Rooms by the hour.
> Or the thrill

Golter was visibly shaking with eagerness. "Maidens are to be...made. Remember?"

"Crude. Just damn crude."

"Do you realize we could be killed? Any day. Don't you want any fun other than killing dragons?"

"What dragons?"

"Well, true. No dragons, so far." Then Golter added, pointing towards the young woman who stepped out of the office, smiling at them. "See, who wouldn't like that?"

She called out in husky voice: "Party time, men. Come in and party."

Mhyo muttered, "What party?"

"I'm always for a party!" Golter started to direct his horse towards the woman. "Let's party."

"The Princess—" The woman had parted her robe to give him a [...]

"But nothing! She'll won't know unless you tell her."

"I couldn't not tell her!" Mhyo's eyes were drawn to the woman who was [...] "I'm a Warrior, and I'm honorable. And would never submit to a woman other than his Princess."

"And if she had thrown herself at your feet you would have refused her."

"I'd protect her from her own passions. Though, being a titled Princess she could not act like that . Titles define."

"Oh, God...the wall! Demon Lizard Parts. Define. Define. Title, title. Who cares. Look at her! She wants to party! We might be dead tomorrow. And you'll be a Virgin at Death. What do you think life is all about?"

"Life is not just lusting after maidens!"

"It certainly isn't just killing invisible, imaginary, non-dragons. Probably no real fire-breathing Terrible Rex Dragons—anywhere! I'll take any ol' maiden in favor of a fire-breathing Drag. The more maidens and less Drags the merrier life would be."

"Warriors must kill our required number," Mhyo muttered under his breath, trying hard to ignore the woman standing there so eager to please.

"Yes, I've heard that before. Haven't I? Quit frankly, your the only Drag around!"

The two of them remained silent for a long Time.

The woman having done her erotic best, disappeared into the Lodge.

[...]

For days the signs continued to announce the House of Nymphs. All promised, in one way or another, sensual adventures beyond the normal experiences of Humankind.

[...]

Promises, oh, wicked promises.

THE EPIC DIALOGS OF MHYO, BY CHARLES NUETZEL

[...]
They saw it from a distance.

HOUSE OF NYMPHS

The Temple House was cut into the side of the rocky cliff. Some mod artist had covered the rock on either side with graphic pictures of—
[...]

[Editorial note: There is no record to indicate when or how Mhyo was seduced into entering the Temple of Love. This fact has been the cause of heated debate concerning the authenticity of the following passages.]

In the corridor, Mhyo was suddenly confronted by a lovely young nymph.
"Oh, warrior," the girl said, grabbing [...] "Oh, mighty warrior, you are so strong. So [...] I want to feel [...] I want to know the [...] Surely you want me like that...."
Mhyo struggled with the raw passions, gulping hard as the woman [caressed?]— The shock of what she was doing [...] created a bolt [of fire] ... down his spine. She knelt there, raw passion burned in her eyes. Her lips parted—
[...]
Escaping one woman only drove him into the arms of another. The [place] was a series of endless

corridors lined with rooms. [Naked?] women were [everywhere].

He was aware of a woman [caressing] him. Her soft lips kept brushing his [....] tongue [...] Her breasts [...] and his [hands] felt the yielding [...]

A strange, sobbing sound uttered from the woman's throat as her lips [closed] about [...] Somehow [he] managed to [...] move from her lovely form. The hot memory of those passionate [...] overwhelming him. Only [his] Mighty powers of [Warrior's Will] helped [Mhyo] to leave.

[Editorial Note: The censor's knife had left very little of the above material in tact. The implications of what actually happened are intriguing. Everything that follows certainly indicates he remained master of his virginity during these first encounters—whatever they may have involved.]

[...]
"No...go away. No, no!" He tossed the hands and forms from him. But they continued to swarm back. "Let me out of here!"

A soft voice seductively whispered: "Come quickly, Mhyo. I'll show you the way."

Blindly, desperately thankful for any help, he let the woman's fingers guide him. Suddenly a door slammed shut.

[...] woman had locked the door.

Mhyo gasp at the very sight of her [...] form. She stood there [...] in front of him. Her [...] were full, their

[...]
Mhyo almost pleaded: "The Princess—"

"Take it from me, bud, no Princess is more of a lady than any of us goddess nymphs."

"She's just a human—"

"I'm not suggesting she isn't!"

"She's pure and innocent and—"

"You believe that? She has the same hunger and passion we're feeling right now."

"Please!" He desperately pushed her [fingers] away from [...]

"Oh, come, bud. You're a fool...enjoy me. Please, enjoy. She'd want the same thing."

"How can you say that. You don't even know her." Again, Mhyo brushed her hand off [...]

"I assure you, right from the mouth of Godwall's mistress, the Princess is no flaky prude. She wants you to [...] and then [...] to her. She doesn't want no fumbling, bumbling fool of a Virgin Warrior to mess up her virginity."

"You're vulgar," Mhyo complained, his eyes feasted on [...] His eyes ravished—

"Come on, bud." The nymph's voice grew excited as it almost sang out the House of Nymph Jingle: "A women wants a super Perfectly Cool Mate with 100% Mega Biting RAMable HD to crash her MemMorE 2 xTaCee. [...] Let us teach you The Way, The When, The Where of Love. Cache Free. We'll educate your HD, with real P & C. Use every A,B, Cee-me Disk. Don't delay! We are the fastest 3X rated programs you'll ever find. We deliver, triple-fast. Never out-dated—once installed we give automatic recharges for Eternity. We're the Super-Duper, House of Nymphs; we give, you take. If our entry level course is just too mild, come back again for extra advanced thrills—No Charge. The Princess will screech out in xTaCee... She'll grab your HD, love your A, B & C! Believe you me, she'll fill her diskette [...] "

The Nymph had somehow come very close and [...] blended against his [...], arching [hotly] forward. Mhyo pushed this perfectly formed, delightfully delicious, voluptuous love nymph's [...] away. "You lie. You don't know what you're talking about."

"I know exactly what I'm talking about. What do you think your Princess does late at night in her private chambers? What seething fantasies does her mind conjure while reading all those endless Romantic Tales about far off places? She is Ready! Believe you me. Remember a Princess is there to be simply taken by the man. The label defines. For what other reason do they exist?"

"To inspire."

"Passion! She's not made of ice."

"To—to protected and—'

"Bull. She isn't a helpless child. She's a Princess. Remember: she is a spoiled brat, used to getting her way; having what she wants, when she wants it. Beware, Mhyo. If you wait too long she may not be there empty-armed, alone, just longing for her foolish Warrior love to take what's his. These Royal types dazzle you with word tricks. You're told to seek the required number of Dragons, real or imagined. Slay dragons if you must, but don't buy into her phantom Walls of Resistances. You will soon learn that Walls are there to be torn, ripped, sliced down to size. Believe you me, mighty Warrior, there is nothing more delicious, more rewarding, more perfect than totally devouring another's flesh with yours."

The goddess suddenly [...] "I'm yours for the taking. So feast! Hungry male animal. Devour the banquet of passion my flesh promises to give. Let me teach you. Learn, damn you, learn!"

A voice screamed, it raged against the room's walls, pounded at Mhyo's ears. For a moment he didn't realize the sound came from his own throat. It was the noise of pure, anguished terror.

"Quiet!" the love nymph pleaded. "In the name of the Walls...be quite." She was nakedly alarmed. Her arms swept the room. "There are others out there...just be quite."

"Let me outta here!" he suddenly screamed.

[...]

Mhyo waited outside the temple until early morning, when Golter staggered though the huge entrance and down the steps. The man was obviously exhausted, but grinned his greetings.

"How long," Golter inquired, coming up to his master, "have you been out here?"

"Long enough. Let's go," Mhyo state, grabbing the man's arm, shoving him towards their waiting horses.

"Hey. You don't have to shove. What's the hurry? How about seconds and...thirds? Surely you enjoyed...you did enjoy...I mean—you—" The man broke off, disgusted. "You didn't, did you?"

"I experienced enough...of that...horrid...place," Mhyo announced, for some reason not willing to admit the truth.

"Did you say horrid or Torrid?"

Silence answered.

"You did find a suitable nymph. Surely. There were enough there to suit any normal guy's most picky desires. Surely you found at least one."

"More that just one." Mhyo shrugged. "They were all delightful."

"Oh, thank all the Gods that Speak. For a moment there I feared you were still...well...that you..."

"I won't admit to anything. One way or the other," Mhyo retorted, moving to his horse with firm determined steps.

"You did do the deed?" Golter pushed, mounting. "You did that. You did. It. Surely."

"I did what I did. And quite enough it was for one night."

"One, two, three?" Golter leaned forward in the saddle. "I had several...well ...lessons, myself. I wanted to explore all flavors, shapes and sizes. I was a willing student to all teacher-nymphs. But...there just wasn't enough Time. How about you?"

"Quite frankly, for me, all such matters are private. And they'll remain so," Mhyo stated, realizing this was his best defense for silence.

"You really can be a pain. Talking about it after the games are over can be even better than the actual events...well, sometimes, that is." Golter shrugged. "That sure was a neat place!"

[...]

Just beyond the valley of the House of Nymphs, they found an old man sitting on a small rock on the side of the road. He looked tattered and dejected; his body was thin and bony, covered in ripped, dirty cloth. A small sign was placed on his lap:

Tired servant offers services for bread.
Food or coin will do.

Mhyo tossed the man a piece of meat.

The beggar glanced up, a weak smile on his scarred lips. "Blessing to you. I see you have survived the love nymphs.

"I survived by avoidance," Mhyo suddenly admitted without thinking.

"Yes," Golter groaned, "I supposed you did. I just knew it!"

The man glanced at Golter. "But you submitted."

"Just as any well bread, foolish, crude minded, everyday loyal servant should. I sure did. But my master, here, is obviously a very moral Warrior. Of fine Breeding...too fine, if you ask me!"

"Yes, a fine Warrior in his Prime. My master was fine and loyal and idealistic. Until he submitted to the Nymphs. They doomed him."

Mhyo immediately paid attention. "What happened?

"The Nymphs just took him—fully. He was seduced at first sight! And he learned fast to play dumb, so they would offer repeat lessons. We stayed for days. I don't know. Maybe he just overstayed his welcome. All he talked about, after that, was taking an advanced course at that College of Love. He was never the same warrior he had been before submitting. The first dragon he met devoured his fine young body in one fast gulp—he was nothing but a quick snack."

The man shrugged, as if to say that was the way of the Land of Speaking Walls.

[...]

"Perhaps," Golter said, rather conversationally, several hours later, "it was good you remained a Virgin. Perhaps."

"Perhaps?" Mhyo didn't want to think about those nymphs. "You doubt that, after what he said?"

"Well, maybe he was lying. Maybe the Dragon was a Super Duper one. Perhaps the Nymphs had nothing to do with his master's defeat. At least that Warrior wasn't a Virgin at Death."

"But dead, quite dead. And dead is final. So we're told."

"Maybe you're right. Maybe not." Golter shrugged, face flushed. "Though that fellow might have been lying. Who can tell lie from truth? Both are words. Words and words. Nothing but words. At least these nymphs were real and their bods certainly hot and passionate in giving their pre-programmed lessons. How could you resist? Surely your self-control is beyond belief."

"I thought of the Princess." Mhyo admitted.

"You'd do that. And it worked. Of course." The man shrugged, as if uninterested. "I suppose if you'd been a married man it would be difference in the House of Nymphs."

"Hardly!" But Mhyo actually shivered.

"The rules change for married Folk. You know that. I know that. What loving father has not in his LifeTime known other women. It is the Nature of men."

Golter was, of course, right. There were Rules for Singles; and Rules for Married Folk. They were totally different. After all, the label defined. Single Male Warrior. Married Male Warrior. Different labels; different defining terms. Once married he'd be a different Warrior. Status was all. Such were the Laws of Godwall.

Perhaps, he wondered, teasing himself with the idea, spending long days in the arms of such lovely, wanton nymphs wasn't really such a bad idea. What lessons they could teach! What a dedicated student he would be. What a magnificent mate he'd become for the Princess. If only he were a different Warrior. He felt a shudder rush through him.

Maybe, someday, after he had Grand Status and Position, a return to the House of Nymphs would be okay. After a few married years with the Princess he would find such a revisit quite desirable.

That, of course, would be for Once Up On Some Other Time.

Golter voice shattered such teasingly delicious thoughts. He cried out, pointing at the sky: "Look at that."

Mhyo looked, saw what was a strange, mechanical object flying high in the sky. It was belching smoke from its tale.

Golter exclaimed: "A Dragon!"

"Hardly,' Mhyo noted, remembering something he had seen in [one of the books he'd read]. "Probably a flying machines. Every inventive Wizard is trying to wiz up such a thing."

"Well, Dragon or not. Will you look at that."

The smoke trailing behind the unidentified flying object started to form words.

The Greatest Wizard of Them All

They came upon him on the mountain that stood before the distant valley of Deathwall, just as the waving mouth had told them they would. The castle was tall, built of starkly trimmed, neatly arranged silvery stone. A deep canyon moat surrounded the tall walls of the stone and brick building; the entrance was open, the drawbridge lowered. They had crossed the bridge and entered the courtyard of the castle to find him standing there before the neatly painted sign that read:

THE GREAT WIZARD
Ask him and he will tell you.
He is All-Knowing and
Wise beyond your petty little, tiny, teeny imaginations.
Seek. Question. Inquire.
The Great Wizard Knows All!
Anything he doesn't know,
You'll have to discover for yourself

He stood there, small, robed in the long purple velvet cloak laced with golden-silver threads, a long white beard treading far below his knees. He was the standard Image of Wizards, Old or New Edition. That wrinkled, yellowed thin face gave the illusion

140

of ancient wisdom. Those sunken eyes were mysterious blue fires. The mouth was a gaping shriveled slit that twisted horribly as it spoke. The high pitched voice formed all words as if overly impressed by their meaning. Gnarled, crinkled bone-fingers coiled in the generous folds of the oversize robe, then twisted through the white hairs of that shaggy beard. And a moment later those very same fingers waved dramatically in the air. Now they pointed dangerously, like a threatening blade, thrusting directly at the two visitors.

"I'm the Great and Mighty Wizard," the Great and Mighty Wizard stated, glaring directly at them, though not moving from his spot in the middle of the large courtyard. "And you are a wonderful Warrior, I see. And if you continue on through this courtyard to the back Entrance—or Exit, depending on which way you are going—you'll be facing even more Dragons than you already have."

"I've found no dragons to slay," Mhyo stated, disgusted.

The Wizard smiled. "Perhaps you have looked in the wrong place. Or the wrong place is where you did not look. Perhaps you seek dragons that are made in shapes you can not recognize. Or you recognize the wrong dragons and never realize that you are slaying dragons when they are paper dragons of great power that...well, see...I can be impressive, too. Words. Convolutions. Dragons. So. What kind of dragons do you seek to do combat?"

"The normal run in the mill dragon will do," Mhyo admitted.

"Even the super normal," Golter volunteered, a bit too generously.

"Normal and super great and powerful dragons to challenge your young and powerful body, to prove what a great Warrior our young man here is? True?"

"True," was Mhyo's quick, honest reply. "Everybody knows that Warriors must slay a required amount of dragons. And I've found none."

"Yes. But small ones? Big ones? Obvious ones? Visible ones? Invisible ones? What kind of dragon would be the most difficult for you to kill?"

"I—"

Golter offered in the bold and brazen manner most befitting a loyal Warrior servant: "Huge, ten, twenty, fifty feet high, with gaping mouth and fangs and with hot fire shooting out of —"

"The normal run-in-the-mill monster dragon, then," the Wizard observed with a slight shrug of his narrow shoulders. "But dragons come in all formats and the ones which are most difficult to slay are those which earn you the most metals. Or to put it another way: to win your required rewards you must slay you required number. Of dragons, of course, that is. Yes, the required dragon count. Is that just about it? For the hand of a Princess?"

Mhyo nodded.

"That computes. Quite nicely, too, I must admit. But then, it always does. Warriors have to come this way to find Deathwall...well, the ones that pass their required number of...er...tests. The roads, of course, as you have noted, are filled with many minor and major challenges to the Warrior Class. All of which, obviously, you have survived. Congrats. My warmest Congrats are yours for the taking. But Dragons....don't worry. You will soon discover your fill of dragons, though they may not be in the form or shape of the famous Terrible Rex. They may not be obvious."

Mhyo demanded: "What kind of dragons will they be? Tell me the truth—"

"With the big T?"

When Mhyo nodded anxiously, the Great Wizard continued: "The big T kind of truth might not be what you are expecting."

"How's that?" Golter wanted to know.

"It involves True meanings and True understanding. The big T kind of True."

"I don't understand what you're talking about." Mhyo objected. "I seek Truth and Understanding— and Dragons and Knowledge of how to become more than I—"

"Yes, yes, of course, you seek understanding. How original. As if you were the first of the People to search for Truth. And...well, what would you think of as being very true? Love? Death? Life? Monsters? Run of the mill Dragons? Walls? Gods? Maybe what is..." He paused, now smiling, eyes shaded in a narrow squint, but twinkling. "Perhaps what is behind the next wall? Well, any wall. The Wall, that is. What is beyond the Walls that Speak? The Cosmos Divine? The Endless Universe? Aliens? Monsters that the mind can not even imagine? The Secrets of Creation? The answers to all the Universal Questions of Why, Where, How, When, What? Is that what you might find beyond the Wonderful Walls that Speak? Maybe the Secret of Time. Perhaps the Answers to Magic. What about The True Laws of Nature? Or, maybe, Origin of All the Folk? Or Other Folk, beyond the Walls that Speak?

Or simply...that there truly is not a thing at all...just the End. Yes, maybe you will discover there is nothing beyond our reality! Is it all illusion? Or, perhaps, you will see the beginnings of the Big Bang. Perhaps the Ending of all Bangs—Big or Small. Black Holes? Worm Holes? Expanding Universes? Or Contracting Universes? What is behind the Walls that Speak? What is beyond the...well...well...whatever?"

"Well...that's a thought. What is beyond the next mountain and thus...I guess, beyond the walls..." The thought intrigued Mhyo; as it had every time he occurred to him. He considered it for some moments.

"Yes, quite an interesting concept, isn't it?" the Wizard stated without so much as a flicker of expression.

"But, of course," Golter put in, "there is nothing beyond the walls."

"So they say," the Wizard agreed.

"The end of the universe," was Golter's next comment. "Nothing?"

"Yes...but if there is nothing beyond the walls...what is that nothing? What is nothing, for that matter? A lack of something? What? Well, consider...some of the People have very little between the walls of their skulls...one might even go so far as to say they had no thing between their ears but a voided space. Or they might have screaming voices telling them all kinds of confusing things, making it impossible to understand anything and thus they might as well have nothing there at all. So...nothing...what is it? Void? Or a confusion of ideas and thoughts and things that simply negate

one another until there is nothing. Is that what is beyond the walls? Assuming there is anything beyond
them?"

Mhyo shook his head in confusion, struggled
and decided to ignore such silly questions.

The Wizard seemed to consider the silence, then
finally said: "Well, as I was pointing out before we
started talking about nothing...What is Truth to you?
What is being very true? Pick a subject. Be my
guest. Pick one. Love? Death? Life? Mons—"

"Love. Certainly that is true and real. I love the
beautiful Princess—"

"Okay. Love. Now there is a very real truth—
with a little 'T'—that can be illusion or real and unreal illusion or really nothing less than illusion. It all
changes, you know. And anything that changes can,
we might wonder, be considered slightly, at the very
least, unreal."

"Then...what is real?" Mhyo demanded, furious,
fighting a non-rational impulse to draw his sword
and cut this Wizard down to size. If that was possible. Of course.

"I am real, and I see you and I can touch you,
talk to you and I can respond to you. But when you
are gone...are either of us real, any more, to the
other?"

"Why," Golter blurted, "of course!"

"Hardly in a real sense. I will think of you as my
mind understood you to be. Of course you will only
continue to thusly exist as long as I live; or until I
might see you again—and then you will be different. And with your mind you will do the very same
concerning me. Nonetheless, it is very possible that

I shall change little, from this Time and any future point of Time when we might again meet."

Golter grunted in open disgust, as was his habit when totally confused.

"In fact, maybe I am more real than either of you because I will change very little. I have changed hardly at all for many hundreds of years, so why should I change much in the future? And if I change little, or not at all, I am as real a creation as I will ever be. So you now surely see reality before you, something that has not, and will not, change very much.

"But I will not exactly be the same from one moment to the next, simply because Time moves through and past me. Or is it that I move through Time? I never could quite get that correct. But never mind.

"My non-changing will make me more real today and tomorrow, for there will be little, if any, difference between me in the future and me at the present. You see, there has been little change in me in the past. Thus I seldom change.

"So I am more real now than you are. For I have changed little and will change little. And don't forget, I have spoken these words many times to young Warriors and their servants. Then, later, when I again see them, they are not the same men I met before, for they have changed. They always say I am the same, for I have not changed, so I have more reality.

"If one changes they become something different, and to become something different is not to be the same thing one was before or will be in the future.

146

"I envy you young ones. You change so much and so quickly. Thus you are more illusion than reality. Once you have lived a little longer, you will come to realize, as I do, that reality is hardly as interesting as illusion. Remember that illusion can take many shapes, but a reality stays the same, boring self for eternity."

Mhyo glanced at Golter and saw the expression of contempt and total lack of understanding. It almost, but not quite, reflected his own feelings. This Wizard was most confusing.

"You both look disappointed," the Wizard observed after a short silence.

"Well," Mhyo admitted, "I did expect some kind of great wisdom. Something that could be of use to—"

"I have said many things. If they are wise or not to you is a matter of your own conscious...experience."

"My experience is frustration!" Mhyo retorted.

"What is it you have come to discover?"

"Well...I thought you were a powerful and great and wise Wizard and—"

"What is it you want from me?"

"Well...what do you offer? Can't you tell me what kind of...dangers—"

"There are many dangers ahead, that is sure. And the only words of wisdom I can really give are: be very fast and remain alert to all kinds of terrible horrors. There are powers that can change you far too fast for your body and mind to adjust to. Remember, instant death is far less desirable than going through death at your own pace. Nobody knows for sure—unless it might be Deathwall, and It will not tell—what is beyond Death."

"Beyond...Death...Deathwall?" Mhyo gasped.

"Remember that a Wall is a Wall and a Wall is there to stop movement . In our Lands of many speaking Walls it is necessary to understand and remember that."

"Oh?"

"Why, of course! I have always wondered, and, since I have changed little in the past century, I have not stopped wondering about the same thing: what might be beyond the Land of Walls. Nothing or some thing? But, of course, as you know, Godwall enjoys playing with riddles about nothings and something. It always tries to convince everybody that being a nothing, a nobody, is better than being a somebody. Remember that once you have become a somebody, and earned your Titles—with a big 'T'—and place, you have actually limited yourself to those grand and wondrous honors. And thus become something of a no thing, and of little importance.

"And what would happen if a fool were to discover there is some thing beyond merely being a something—as Godwall and Deathwall may surely be. And what if one were to learn what was beyond the Walls—like what is beyond the sky? Maybe nothing, but if it is something, according to Godwall, it surely must be a nothing."

"That doesn't make any sense!" Golter fairly shouted.

"It just does not make much sense, but then, that is the Paradox of Walls and the very point of the riddle of life. If there is a point; and sometimes I wonder about that, too. If nothing is beyond the Walls...and if something is beyond the Walls...what is that something/nothing? Is it terrible and danger-ous beyond our imagination? Thereby the greatest giant dragon to slay? Or is it beautiful peace and without warring creatures and destroyers who would be worshipped as Deities of Dogma? Or just more confusion and conflict? And would life, or whatever it might be called, beyond the Walls be worth the experiencing? Total peace might be like total death—no conflicts and no life. For surely the proc-ess of living is a process of confusion and much like the experience we all share in this land between the Walls that Speak. All things seem to have their lim-its. Except for the Process of Discovery. Godwall says: the discovery can at times be a dud—oh, but the search, the chase...that's something else."

"What's so wonderful about that?" Golter wanted to know.

"Is there a woman who does not understand the challenge of mystery and the excitement of the chase? As long as the mysterious shimmer of cloth-ing restricts the view, as long as there are monsters to defeat and escape, silken walls to block the way, we have the adventure of attempting to dis-cover...the thrill of winning. But once the prize is ours, well...we sometimes realize that the price we have paid is a bit more costly than the prize is worth. If we reverse that with a little mind-magic, we can discover that the price we pay to gain our goals is sometimes much too high. On the other hand, it can be true that the cost is worthy of the rich rewards."

"Don't make sense to me!" Golter moaned, shaking his head slowly from side to side.

"Once we own the mine we can dig all its gold out and then...what? We have nothing, nothing but the experience and naked rock."

"Then you are saying that the experience itself is sometimes worth more than the end result?" Mhyo suggested, bemused.

"I am saying that Godwall points this out. The experience is the reward. Think back, did he not tell you to consider the distance between the beginning and the end of your journey might be more important than the actual destination—the final ending?"

"But," Golter asked, "is there an ending?"

"A very pointed question. Like I said, if you wish reality: never change. If you wish illusion: move through the Process of continued change and you will never be real. To finally be real you must stop changing—and, sadly, grow old and die, given Time...and that is certainly a form of decadent change. But in our land Time is a strange thing, it moves and we move and it is all one and different and no point of Time is less meaningful than the other. Nor is it more important. Nor more real. When it has passed, when it is gone, it is nothing but a memory. It is an illusion of reality that our minds have distorted into the shape and form we wish to perceive. This is not true reality, either.

"I am not what you think me to be any more than you are what I think you to be and none of us are what we think of ourselves to be."

"Then what are we? What are you?" Mhyo countered.

"Well, I am what I am. I have had much time to think about what I am. It is more likely I am more real than you. Certainly I have greater understanding about all matters small and large. Thus my conclusions are certainly sounder than yours. My conclusions have been set for Billions of your years. And they have never changed. Nor have I. Well, not much, that is. At least I have never changed in the last hundred of my years. So...as I say, I am real, you are illusion ever-changing into new illusion in its search for reality, which would be much like me, only different.

"So...what is beyond the World of Walls? What is real? Is there something or nothing and what is illusion and real? Or what is a wise man or fool?"

"And that is?" Golter ventured.

"Simply consider and maybe you will discover."

Mhyo offered in disgust: "That to be real is not to change and to be illusion is to change. And you say that it is better to be real and not change! It does not make sense."

"Who said anything about making sense?"

"I wished knowledge and got—"

"I have given you all the knowledge I can learn; and that is why I am more real than you. Why is that? you might ask. Well, because I have no more knowledge and know I will learn none beyond what I now know. I am thus real."

Set in stone!

Somehow all had circled back to the beginning and it was obvious that there could be no more that this Wizard would reveal—or, at least, was willing to reveal. Which was, no doubt about it, the same thing.

Mhyo directed his horse around the Wizard. He wondered if upon returning to this spot he would truly discover the same impossible to understand creature. Should that happen, it would, in a way, prove that not changing was being more real than changing.

As they approached the back entrance to the courtyard, Mhyo could see for the first time the other side of the world of walls. It was his first vision of the long awaited destination. The journey was truly coming to a conclusion. The Wall lifted upwards into the sky, disappearing in to the clouds. He also saw in the darkened clouds a huge temple where Deathwall loomed.

A shiver rushed through him.

They slowly left the castle, crossed the black bridge that hung over the moat. Here they could see that the road lead down toward the distant valley below. It was, strangely, a lovely, huge green area of rolling hills, reaching into the distance to the Temple of Deathwall.

Golter suddenly blurted out, quite nervously: "No dragons down there. Surely there are no more...well... obvious dangers to face."

"I suppose you're right about that," Mhyo agreed. It made sense that the Territory immediately surrounding Deathwall might be sterile of real dangers. He turned to face his loyal friend.

It was apparent, in the very first glance, that Golter was ill-at-ease. Even the servant's horse seemed to hesitate, wanting to pull back, away from the path, as if to turn and race back to the lands of Godwall. Golter said nothing, but those eyes silently stated it all.

152

Mhyo Janton, after a moment of prolonged consideration, said: "You must return home, now. As you see, the Road to Deathwall is before me, and there are no obvious dangers. There is nothing at Deathwall for you. Godwall said nothing about you facing this Holy Terror of the Lands."

Golter quickly objected, as was his preprogrammed duty: "But—"

"You were told to serve me. Serve me now by returning to tell Princess Gianni that I found no dragons on my way to Deathwall, but that I continued on. If I don't return then you can tell her that I tried and failed with honor. There is no real reason for both of us to fail. You have proven yourself a worthy servant. And didn't Godwall say that was enough for you to be?"

Golter nodded, hiding his obvious relief.

"Then continue being one. Serve my Princess if she so desires. Serve your maiden. And have many children. There must be future generations in the Lands to continue to serve the Gods and Wizards and Lords and Kings."

Golter started to say something but Mhyo spurred his own horse toward the pathway that led down to the final valley of Deathwall.

"I must face Deathwall alone—and defeat any dragons it might have to conjure up against me. Good-bye...friend."

With that parting statement he focused all attention to the coming final conflict.

DOOM, DESTRUCTION, AND DEATHWALL

Mhyo Janton, during the days that followed Golter's exit, had felt little real fear until actually approaching the temple surrounding Deathwall. The huge valley through which he had gone, after leaving the Great Wizard's Castle, had been endless gardened green lawn, with distant trees lining the horizon at left and right.

Now he moved to the huge arched entrance to Deathwall. Strangely enough there was not much visible difference between this temple and the one that surrounded Godwall, other than a silent suggestion of Doom, a quite cold of Death. That was probably part imagination. There was just the suggestion of darkness clouding the upper reaches of the Temple.

The road led directly into the inner courtyard, huge and empty, except for the white wall that faced anyone entering. In the upper corners shadowy cob webs gathered. From the wall itself the voice sounded in a deep, booming roar.

"You have dared to come all the way!" it accused.

"I have come the full distance to face you," Mhyo managed, voice firm, though he felt very real terror eat at the pit of his stomach.

154

"But you have a Voice—at last! Before Godwall you had no voice at all."

"And the courage to face whatever you represent—and to learn from you want I have come to learn."

"You wish to learn, then?"

Deathwall's words filled the depressive chamber with a threat of overwhelming danger. Though it wasn't in the sound of Its voice; that seemed flat, unmoved, at this point. Rather something far more vague lingered in this place. There was a gloomy sense of shadows, without darkness; a feel of danger, without any obvious show of weapons; an atmosphere thick with threatening horror, yet clear in its visual details. What was visible offered little comfort: the white sheen of the smooth wall was featureless; only those lacy, gathering of webs defaced its surface. It was the invisible that threatened so silently, so secretly, so blatantly. The visual was overwhelming, deadly; yet what hide behind that outer shell was totally different; it was this that loomed so powerfully obvious. The unseen promised doom, destruction and death. It was the hidden power that became far more terrible than what was visually defined.

"Tell me this, what is the purpose of all life?"

"To live, enjoy?" Mhyo suggested, still frightened, but fighting a sense of mystification. This was not quite what he had expected from Deathwall. Nor was Its retort.

"Wrong answer. It is to die! The purpose of all life is to Die! All things are born for dying. It is that simple. All roads lead to me, one way or the other. Have you not listened to the voices on your journey? Have they not pointed that out? Are you not a Warrior dedicated to the destruction of life? Does not a Warrior kill, bring death, serve at the very steps of my temple? Tell me that."

"I was trained to kill, that is true...but to protect. That is the difference."

"Oh. That is the difference. Let me see. To kill in the noble ideal of protection is something different from killing for the pure joy of bringing the final end to life. There is a vast difference! Of course. You would have fit nicely into the Histories of Man. How many of the People are killed merely for the protection of others? In the name of Godwall...or, for that matter, in the name of any other Deity the People might have conjured up out of their desperate need to have Great & Grand Masters to follow? How sad, how strange, how stupid! How blind and...well, the People and their Many Folk gods; their many Folk religions; their many Folk beliefs. How silly. They look for SuperNatural parents to help define themselves. They plead for New Gods to worship in order to understand the purpose of their existence. They lay their lives down in this Total and Complete Blind-Faith Worshipping, and believe that Eternity, Immortality depend on their specially designed religious order. And they would kill to defend their concept of the so-called Truth of Nature, the Truth of Reality. They create their illusions and fantasies into false Institutions. They give their 10,15, 20 percent—or all—to these Cult Chapters. The bow to father-this mother-that. Thus they believe this bought the Insurance to Life-After-Me! Hah! They believe too much! How dare they make-believe such rot? How dare they deny the True Reality that is here and now in the Land of Walls that Speak?" Deathwall paused, as if catching Its breath. Then Deathwall continued: "We were saying that killing is, of course, evil, terrible, wicked, against the very Nature of all Gods real or imagined. How there is godly purpose in killing, or no purpose at all other than the pleasure of death and destruction. You were suggesting there must be some noble purpose in the taking of life; and I was pointing out how un-noble all such purpose. I simply wished to say the People are mad! They kill for grand and mighty purposes all of their own design. It is really quite a laugh, when I consider all True Reality. The People serve their gods and go forth to gain converts for these many make-believe Cult Orders. Others who refuse to believe are forced to fight, and even die, for the privilege of not believing. Why, it is horrid to kill without Grand & Noble purpose. So they say."

Then, with only a slight pause, It added in a voice dripping raw with mockery: "It is, of course, perfectly okay and moral to kill with noble purpose. Especially in the name of one's...whatever. Then, of course, that makes everything right and proper."

"To battle for food, survival and love is what living is all about. Even more honorable is to fight for one's Deity, in the name of one's God. For what higher purpose could a Warrior have to fight but in the defense of such things?" Mhyo wanted to know.

"Higher?" the Voice of Deathwall cried, bombing through the large room. "Where have I spoken about higher purpose? There is no higher or lower purpose. There is only one purpose that serves my needs for being. All purposes are the same for all roads end at the same destination. All come here at one point of Time or another.

"And it is always the Now for that which dies. All reality is in the Now. All else is illusional memory, recorded awareness of what one has observed while passing through what we call Time. Or fantasy dreams of what might be at some future Time. But death comes in our mental/physical Now. And to what ever perverse purpose death might serve to others it only serves one purpose to me: the final and complete reason for birth. How can one have death without birth? Creation. Existence. And. Death. The circle completed. Before life was nothing and after death what else could they be but nothing? The circle is completed."

"Why must the circle be completed?"

"An incomplete circle is something other than a circle. All is circles, anyway. Consider: Non-life, birth, existence, death, non-life. All back to the same. All roads lead to Deathwall. How else could it be in the Lands?"

"What of immortality?" Mhyo challenged, by now frustrated by all Dogma.

"All things die."

"You have not died."

"What is dead cannot live; what has never lived can not die."

"You live."

"I represent Death. I am the end of the journey for all living matter. I exist."

"You exist and thus must live."

"What do you know of such matters? Okay, my young Warrior friend, I'll suggest a possible illustration to you: let us say you could destroy me. What would happen?"

"You would be dead."

"But I am Deathwall! I am, if the word applies at all, already dead—or at least the ultimate conception of Death and Destruction. I can not be made more of what I am than I now am."

"But what if I could destroy you?"

"And how would you go about destroying Deathwall?"

"Well...I don't know. But...what if I wanted to see beyond you—discover what it is you hide. For walls are nothing but objects to block movement or hide something—"

"You would then—I guess—have to find some way to kind of destroy my power over you. That is true. But you would then discover something so terrible that your mind could not accept what it saw. And since I am already the symbol of total Death, I could not be totally destroyed...death is death. Death is unchanging, thus real. Life ever-changing, thus is momentary illusion."

It made one of Its dramatic pauses, as if to underscore this last point. Finally, once the message had sunk in, It continued: "But, perhaps, could there not be something beyond me—something more terrifying than what I represent? Something that would cause you to embrace Deathwall rather than face that other place? Could it be that in such a way I serve Man, by walling-off what the People are frightened to know? Consider the possibility that I am here for that purpose...along with many other grand and mighty purposes, all of which are meant to simply serve the People."

"Like...what?" Mhyo demanded, thankful for the delay in any possible Battle to the Death.

"Like, without me, how could there be war? Grand and small?"

"Well..."

"War without killing would be dumb to the People. So, I'm of value; I'm important, with human purpose, if you like."

"That is...well..."

"You sound puzzled. So let me put it this way: You humans—to say nothing of all the living creatures in the universe—serve in worship of me in almost all things. You fear me and yet you purposely let my powers be used for your own petty goals. Gaining of: land, more riches, conquering; taking from others. Most terrible: inflicting your religious and political ideals on all within reach. Believe my dogma or die! Why, you could not even live without killing. You kill animals for their flesh, you plant and grow and harvest and eat vegetation, which is, surely, life, too. There is no way for you to exist without serving me. You claim to serve Godwall, with his words of creating and purpose and moral value, but in the end you pervert such ideals and grand forms in total worship of myself, Deathwall. You must do this in order to survive and continue experiencing your Now Existence as long as possible."

"Why?"

"Because you realize, against all willingness to do so, that you will ultimately face me. Thus this fear of me is a kind of instant to instant worship."

"But—"

"But nothing! Consider the more basic moves, the grand and wonderful purposeful Games of War. Oh, how delightful they are. Mass killing in the name of...what ever you wish to use as an excuse: love, survival, greed, religious, political...whatever. And you continue to say that Humankind does not worship me? Or that a professional Warrior is not my personal servant? All roads lead to Deathwall. Never forget that."

"Unless one learns how to overcome, and if that is not possible then to pass beyond you; or refuse your very power to destroy—"

"Or, like the snake said, 'Go backwards to Godwall, but then it would send you forward, which might be backwards, and then you would not know if you were coming or going—which is the state of most of the People.' But. There have been a few who have tried to pass and/or see beyond me. They have tried. Madness. But it has been done, I'll have to admit that. A few have even seen beyond me...for a short moment. That was more than enough. Much more than they could cope with. Some have even gone beyond, rather than through, me. They call it transcending. But—"

"What?"

"No matter what you call it, how you do it, the method must involve embracing that which I represent. You must overcome the fear, the terror. Experience the total form of destruction. You must have the willingness to face your own self-destruction. Be willing to transcend all the emotional and intellectual fears and rationalizations and...well, whatever! Combat with me will certainly bring you defeat. For I represent total destruction;

161

death. How could you survive that? And if you did...what would be the end result? The experience could bring you madness and a kind of certain self-destruction totally unimagined in your present, glorious state."

A dramatic Deathwall pause, then: "You see, even then you risk the ultimate price-tag: death. So all roads do end at the same place. Me!"

"How, then, does one take that ultimate move forward? How does one engage you? How does one ...transcend or by-pass you?"

"Engagement, total willingness to engage whatever I might be, whatever I might represent and thus take the chance of risking total destruction. One must be willing to take this kind of total risk in order to even have the chance of seeing beyond me. Most, of course, are not willing. They might learn who they really are, what the Lands of the People truly are, what the all this confusion truly is...in this land of illusional reality. They may, suddenly, have their chance to look past the illusion and see the reality. Most would rather avoid such Reality and merely deal with the illusion. Embrace the Mystical rather than accept the real truth. Worship false Ideals rather than fully embrace what is all around them and in them and a part of them and ...well, perhaps is them. Are you willing to totally take that final peek? Are you willing to reach into me, let me crush your total existence? I could smash your inner and outer Soul. I could shred your mind to nothingness. Or expand it until it explodes. Want to embrace my very existence? Are you ready to submit to the force of my Truth? Are you willing to become more than you have ever been?"

"I am a Warrior and I am here to learn and I am here to be totally dedicated to what I am."

"Not more than you are?"

"Maybe the only way to discover that or the difference, the real from the unreal, is to totally engage you with everything I am aware of being."

"That might cause a lot of undesirable stress, you know. And stress is considered by the most wise and learned Doctors to be a very sneaky, Silent Killer. Sorta my kinfolk. Are you truly ready for such a challenge?"

"A challenge to a Warrior is nothing short of a demand for action."

"So I've noticed in most cases when Godwall sends Warriors to me with the puzzle of discovering how to be more than they are—most accept illusion rather than face the real challenge. Most have not listened to the right voices. Some have been willing to merely do as others suggest. Many can't tell the real dragons from the illusional ones. You seem willing to meet your own purpose regardless of what others might or might not have suggested or told you."

"I have learned to wave my arms and my mouth!" Mhyo snapped, determination finally setting his muscles into tight knots. He reached for his sword, pulling it out, set in his saddle, feet braced, shield firmly locked protectively in place, prepared for whatever engagement might follow.

"Action and words. Still limiting. You go up against Deathwall with the action of total worship to my purpose—it hardly seems to indicate your own purpose. Apparently you have not, as yet, learned you own purpose."

"You speak words. Well, I am a Warrior. I know how to be a good Warrior. Yet, I do not worship you as my deity. Nor will I concern myself with Godwall's riddles, for I've learned there is no way of being more than I am. Merely being what I am is important and the only way I can do that is by being willing to discover what that is—nothing more or less. As was suggested, Warriors war...! Lovers love. I am both. Wizards wiz. Walls that speak are nothing but speaking walls. Their label defines, and limits, them. If I must, I will do battle as best I can against whatever force or power you can bring to bare against me. It is the most I can do—anything less would be being less than I am. It is not important being more than I am, I can never become more other than through discovery, growth. Perhaps the snake was right, to be more than I am I merely have to eat more—but not necessarily food. Be willing to experience and thus become more within my own experience."

"At least you have learned to speak far better than you did before Godwall. Then you had no voice—or not much of one. I see that your experience, what you have gone through during your journey here to me, has given you a grand and mighty voice. Yes...you are quite right, experience can make you more than you were. But how do you plan on dealing with me? With a sword? Against death rays?"

Mhyo knew he did not have the answer to that question. But he must deal with Deathwall. One way or the other. It was the only chance he had to learn what might or might not be beyond It. What mysteries, what secrets, did It block? Where did the road lead beyond Deathwall? What did It defend? Most of all, why was It there in the first place? .

"Perhaps," Mhyo suggested, "my sword will prove quite enough to shield me from all your super destructive forces."

"And you are determined to find out...one way or the other?"

"I am a dragon slayer who has found the only dragon worth slaying," Mhyo stated. "My fear of you and what you refuse to reveal."

"What about your lovely Princess..."

"She will be there when I return. I can not return until I have finished what it is I have come to do."

"And if you do not survive?"

"I can do nothing about that, can I?"

"You can turn, leave, go back the way you came, accept the Land of Walls. Golter was happy to return, glad to get off the hook. He had a normal, very human fear of what I represent."

"I won't judge others—I only know what I must do. Right or wrong has nothing to do with my desire to totally face you. If I have learned nothing more than dragons come in totally different casts and shapes and sizes, I have learned much. If I under-stand that most demons and dangers come in invisi-ble patterns, and that a true warrior must slay only those that represent a true threat, I have learned more than I could have expected. That is another way of learning how to become more than I was."

"More than you were," Deathwall mockingly corrected.

"And in whatever manner possible deal with you" Mhyo's voice grew louder as he concluded:

"That's what I'm here for—and I won't leave until one of us is defeated."

"As you wish!" Was Deathwall's quite verbal response. "So, let use begin."

DEATHWALL REVEALED

Without warning a ray, white as starlight, shot directly at Mhyo's head.

His shield automatically lifted.

Another ray shot out.

His sword swung in a terrible effort to cut—or block—that death-light. The first exchange was so rapid, so unexpected, that he did not have a chance to do more than react. All took place in total silence.

As moments passed, and no third bolting ray attack, Mhyo slowly lowered his shield.

He noticed two charred black holes in the wall in front of him. They cut deep into the smooth facing of Deathwall.

"Well?" Mhyo shouted, feeling a surge of power. He had survived—so far.

"Well?" came a calm voice from Deathwall.

"Well—what?" he countered in sudden doubt.

"I have but tested your courage," Deathwall announced coldly. "And...well you have that, for sure. You are more than just words, more than a mouth waving itself. More than a snake in the pond double-talking about roads that lead back and forth. You have at least, if nothing else, stubborn courage. But what is it you expect to see beyond me? What is it that you believe I block? Why should you bother to concern yourself with such matters? Would it not be easier to simply go back and claim your Princess?"

"I could—for she would believe whatever I told her. But I want to know the truth. I won't hide in that slimy green pool in the illusion of being safe. I don't desire to accept the concept that reality is nothing but not changing; or that to not change is to be more real than continuing to change through growth. I won't accept lies. I now know I could have had my Princess for the mere taking of the prize as she stood their in front of her chamber's door. A Princess like all others will follow those who have the guts to conquer and claim their rewards by the pure power of what they are. And I also know one can not have what is not already theirs. She was mine from the beginning. The point is sometimes not to define but to outline. Yes...I have leaned to listen and accept. My process is to gain what ever purpose and object my total abilities are able to claim. I know the Paradox of Walls. It is the confusion of many voices, the treadmill of endless riddles. I wish nothing less than discovering the final secret, the true reality. I am not interested in illusion. I wish reality."

"Then, as Godwall suggested, you wish too much!" Deathwall exploded.

"By whose' standards? Godwall's? Yours? Or mine?"

"And your standards are?"

"If it is possible, I will discover all I can. If it is possible I will survive that discovery. And I believed it is possible to build my own walls, and not depend on those that others place before me to obstruct my vision and view."

168

"Oh, then you would claim whatever fate—no matter what the price—and accept total responsibility for your actions? And the results of your actions?"

"I survived your first attack. Perhaps I can survive your next one. If you dare to make it."

Mhyo pointed with his sword at the two holes in the side of the wall. Huge black pits burned into what had been silvery white. "The reflection of your own destructive form?"

Silence answered him. To Mhyo that silence was answer enough to his question. The only way to deal with Deathwall was to let Its own force be used against It, to reflect Its power back onto Itself. One could not kill Deathwall, that was true, It could not be more than It was; but It could be forced to feed upon Itself, to become Its own destruction.

The rays shot out at once, from left, right and high up, streaming directly at Mhyo. The air crackled with blue light.

Mhyo's sword flashed, cut at the right ray, shield blocked the other two laser flashes.

This time, though, his attention was partly on what happened as a result of his defensive moves. The rays refracted, returning at right angles, striking the walls of the Chamber of Deathwall, burning huge holes. All such destruction was harmless to the Deity of Death.

"You see, young Warrior, it is not quite as simple as you might have thought.."

Mhyo considered and merely said: "Do you merely wave words in the air? No? Then you must be willing to be what you are, the total demonstration of destruction for the sake of destruction. You must face the fact that I have discovered the secret of defeating you!"

There was nothing more than a thoughtful pause, then light flashed. Pulsating beams streamed at Mhyo.

He held his shield firmly in place. He calmly observed, sword ready to strike rays coming from other directions. His mind calculated. He lifted the shield so that the rays splattered against it, causing them to reflect back. This time the rays sprayed across the surface of Deathwall.

It happened faster than Mhyo expected. A charred line exploded along the back of Deathwall. Two rays beamed at his head, but Mhyo effortlessly returned them with his sword. They bounced off the blade.

In a matter of moments the battle had ended. The face of Deathwall smoldered; It was a series of crumbling black holes. Illusion? Reality? It did not matter any more to Mhyo. He had challenged and proved worthy of the resulting battle.

Yet, what happened next was totally unexpected.

BEYOND THE WALLS AND BACK

For a flickering moment the walls crumbled along with Deathwall. All of them shimmered and then vanished and he could see beyond.

The illusion, the reality blurred in his mind.

He was floating in Eternity.

A fantasy image flickered behind the haze, showing distant circles and circles of walls, all of different sizes, all drifting into the infinity of space, like other worlds, other beings. Then these seemed to pulse away, becoming mere twinkling stars. They gathered together into swirling masses. After a moment blackness swallowed it all up, distorted the images. Color flashed in bright rays, images flickered, strange lands, strange settings, none defined enough to form actual pictures. Nothing connected. It almost seem as if he were becoming aware of other minds, other thoughts, other consciousness. But everything was vague, out-of-focus. The blurred forms abruptly gathered together, reformed into Circles of Walls. He stared, stunned. He simply had the illusion of other...what? Creatures of different Universes? Or things like himself? Illusion? Real? It was difficult to even be sure that he could really see beyond the walls. How could he know what was real, what was not?

Then quite suddenly the natural barrier between here and there reformed, as if unwilling to non-exist, no matter how much destructive force reflected back at It.

Deathwall had cracked, vanished, and now returned

Deathwall was in place as a natural construct between Mhyo and that strangely populated dark dimension of other places, other Times, other Realities. That Infinity was safely cut off by the Walls that Spoke. The Universal Answers to all Questions Why had retained their haunting mystery.

Deathwall ignored him.

He ignored Deathwall.

Having removed Its image for even that instant proved It could be defeated. If once, why not again?

Deathwall did not matter, now. It had no power over his existence. It could continue to play Its silly games with the other People of the Land of Walls. Mhyo knew what he was and was not. He knew far more than he wished to understand; and far less than he wished to totally know. So, perhaps, some other Time would be soon enough to force Deathwall to go away...

In order for a person to grow it was necessary to expand their understanding to the final limits. Had he not shown his willingness to look beyond the Walls that Spoke? Even for a glimmering moment?

That was enough—for this Time!

Like any good Warrior general, he knew when to back off, stop. Now he needed Time to think, plan. More importantly, he wanted a moment to enjoy the rewards of a hard won victory.

He would play out the game and go back to Godwall and offer himself a title; and he would embrace his Princess. He had learned that much. He had learned that in his momentary vision of what lay beyond Deathwall. He would return here at some other Time and step beyond this Wall. He would once again look at the billions of other Circles of Walls that went off into the infinity. Maybe communication would be possible, maybe he would be able to learn from those other circles. Maybe he could make contact with them. But not this Time.

Then he considered all that was around him, all that had happened, and realized that he did not even need to seek out Godwall. It had no more power over him than Deathwall demonstrated. Whatever had created all that was certainly wasn't Godwall. It had no power other than what the People gave It. This God of all Walls could only form grand and mighty sounding words. Any power It might seem to have was Illusional. Mhyo now knew he did not need to get Its permission, nor Its approval, for anything.

He could almost imagine himself standing before Godwall, telling it to "bug off!"

He realized that with Godwall it would be necessary to define and outline and play games, wear masks, run in circles, and be much like the snake who talked about the confusion of directions.

He shrugged off such ideas.

He considered the vision he had seen.

What might they be? Those Circles of Walls? Much like the wall that circled his illusional reality? Maybe those other circles were nothing more than other illusional realities. Perhaps they were other

Worlds of Speaking Walls. Other Consciousness, seeking Truth, Wisdom, Knowledge.

He muttered half aloud to himself, in better understanding: "All are masks, all are merely different parts of the total. Maybe even I, myself, am nothing more than a portion of the total reality. Maybe all that is around me is nothing but a part of the whole that is the total me. Perhaps I do not wish to reach beyond that self until I've learned to understand my own land of illusional reality. Or maybe within this ring of walls is enough stuff to satisfy my craving for self-awareness and self-experience. Maybe, most of all, it would be foolish to reach beyond the Circles of Walls until I have found full awareness, full experience, full understanding and full love for this which is me. I will think for a while about such matters. I will experience what is here and now offered. I will search for true love and greater fulfillment with my own dream Princess, who is mine for the mere acceptance.

"How does one become more than they are? It is a fool question spoken by a false, illusional god and best answered by eat a lot. We never become more than we are at any Time, we merely recognize and accept that the true and only method is to understand what we are. Growth comes with change; change makes us something more than we were."

He turned his horse and directed it through the rubble that had remained as a result of the final conflict with Deathwall.

"My journey is ended. For now. This Now. This Time." Someday, Mhyo realized, he might to back for a Second Challenge to Deathwall.

But for now, in this Once Up on a Timer, he had to face the return journey that would take him back to so many interesting places. So many missed chances, miss opportunities. A second chance to explore the total possibilities that he had so foolishly avoided. Golter had been right about his obsessions. Dragons were defined by events; and they were never quite as obvious as any ol' Terrible Rex. He had resolved the Dragon issue by defeating Deathwall. He had, Mhyo decided, killed his required amount—and then some. It was now okay to be less rigid concerning what was right and wrong. Titles only defined if you let them. Rules by false gods were to be ignored.

The return trip certainly offered new possibilities.

This Time around, being a somewhat different Warrior, he must take more advantages of what was offered for free in this wonderful, beautiful Lands of Living Walls that Spoke.

Regardless of the details of these experiences, whatever they might have been, they certainly do not belong to this present adventure. All that counts is that he returned to his Princess. It is enough to say, at this point, that, as with all good fairy tales, this one must end with:

And they lived happily ever after.

HISTORICAL NOTE

[As offered in the surviving Historical Documents on which this present edition is based.]

The "Happily ever after" part seems to have been quite real. All existing records imply that Mhyo returned to his Princess and they had many children.

There is even one strange, obscure, text telling of a long visit to the Temple of the Goddess Nymphs, where he learned the arts of love. Since most experts feel this to be the fictional imaginings of some pornographic writer, it is being ignored in all official publications concerning the Myth. Nevertheless there is implied evidence in some ancient records and scrolls that a warrior very much like Mhyo, though not mentioned by name, dedicated some Time to getting the "required amount" of experience necessary be a skilled lover. (Certainly there is no record of any complaints from the Princess.)

One would like to believe that he became a famous dragon killer and more importantly a Master Sage, as one, literally "off the wall" ancient scribbling states concerning "The Warrior"—though does not name him. This person authored many books, the most famous being THE BOOK OF

SAYINGS FROM THE WORLD OF WALLS AND ITS PARADOXES. How can one tell fact from fiction, myth from make belief? All such records are frustratingly vague. There is no actual written evidence of his returning to Deathwall, though surely he did die, given the correct Time.

The only existing intact document of his adventures are those found in the little shop in India and published here.

There are lists of his writings; little else but short quotes in other ancient documents. His name is mentioned in other text, which does little more than established his fame during some pre-ancient period.

Perhaps, at a future date, a new discovery, in another tiny shop, somewhere on the planet Earth, will turn up, and even relate some other Once Up on a Timer.

We can only hope.

EPILOG

A few words concerning this book:

If you are a True Believer in fables and Gods and Wizards—and such stuff—then you must be faithful to yourself and not read the following Author's explanation.

At least no further until you have finished the *Epic Dialogs*. The *Epic* is something totally different from anything I have written and I had for many years simply considered it a non-commercial experimental bit of writing which most authors end up playing around with at one time or another. I think I broke "all the rules" at the very beginning and never quite got back on a so-called commercial track. *The Dialogs of Mhyo* all came out of a lot of notes jotted down over a period of years and finally converted into a Q&A dialog of such boring content that I realized it was necessary to beef it up by making a couple of fictionalized characters dialog with one another, within the structure of some kind of plot. Sadly I was not fascinated with the idea of writing a novel, so it ended up as a 20,000 word manuscript dealing in a somewhat limited and stilted way with the basic core of the *Dialogs* (conversational exchanges between different characters devised to mouth my magnificent words of wisdom!).

Well, it rotted in my files, tormenting me for some ten or more years. I even revised it from time to time, but never could discover what to do with it. I tried cutting it, and while that brought about amazing improvements and simplified some of the complications and convolutions, the silly thing still refused to become a magnificent commercial bit of writing. Sometimes a writer does something that pleases himself, but nobody else. That was the problem: I was in "love" with the basic material, and the more I worked with it the better the whole thing became—but still all in all wasn't quite right.

The solution, of sorts, came during a long e-mail exchange with Charles A. Gramlich, another writer, over a period of almost a year. I mentioned the Epic manuscript and ended up getting creatively wound up again, this time with a concept of what could perhaps work. I would CUT the blasted Epic down, even while adding fresh material, a plot-line and sub-plot material. Heck, I ended up cutting a 20,000-word manuscript "up" to almost 40,000 words, in a fever of creative fury. My wife would hear me giggling or laughing in my office, before the computer, and wondered what was happening. She found it difficult to understand that I would be laughing at my own material. Well, if it don't amuse de author it ain't gonna amuse de reader. Not smart to write somethin' which ain't funny even to de writer!

Well, I enjoyed much of the material and hopefully figured others might enjoy. So, once again it is offered up not as an example of wonderful writing, but of a writer's creative self-indulgence, and egomania! Then just a few days ago I was exchanging emails with a woman who I've known for some time, Heidi Garrett, and because she was one of the very first of the few who have read the Epic, I shared my concept for the cover.

After offering the required number of compliments concerning the cover, she added: "You're right—I always liked the recoiling snake—know that one well. I was also very aware that the columns came from your Egyptian travels—wondering why you chose the Roman columns as opposed to Greek or the original Egyptian which would have dated back to a much older time, since Mhyo is supposedly older than all of them—just my question...Heidi."

To which I replied: "Where do you think the Romans got their ideas? You know how things cycle. Well. Those kinds of columns existed many a thousands of years previously; as you can see! Well, also, you really forget the totality of the *Dialogs* and what they are truly all about, and where they are taking place. Remember?

"Somewhere in the mind of the reader—for that's what it is all about: the world of walls is the totality of our minds! And all the creatures therein are inventions of our very inner selves, the voice within our minds, doing their battle, seeking dragons to slay. But in reality such creatures or phantoms within our own mental universe, are mere shadows within shadows. And wizards and snakes are nothing more than symbolic inventions we create to mystify ourselves into thinking we are something other than what we are, or simply to confuse our very awareness of all things."

As to Walls that Speak, especially of the God &
Death kinds of walls, they are nothing more but
imagined barriers between our inner selves and that
which lies beyond our awareness, lives, existence.
The world of walls is, to me, a reflection of all the
conflicting voices and desires and passions and in-
ternal battles that go on within ourselves. And we
can never get beyond the walls as long as we let our
own belief that there are godwalls and deathwalls
and speaking walls that simply reflect the continued
thoughts bouncing off themselves.

Mhyo finally did battle with that most deadly
and frightening wall of all—Deathwall—and over-
came it by reflecting its own destructive force
against itself, and for a moment got a peek into what
lay beyond it, what it had been attempting to keep
from him, what he had been hiding from. I suppose
you could say that the *Dialogs* is just one example
of how things are for one being who struggled to
become more than he was only to discover that he
had to go outside of himself...and when he looked
out there he was so frightened by what he saw that
he turned away in horror, willing to face the demons
and devils and dragons within the confines of his
own soul and learn to conquer that within himself,
his sense of right and wrong, his sense of self and
worth and coming to the understanding that words
may define and titles may shade, but none of it in
reality restricts. We are what we let ourselves become.

Mhyo didn't have to deny himself of what was
already his, all he had to do was go back and claim
his rights, to claim all that he was. And one of those
things, certainly, was the right to love and be pas-

sionate and to be able to experience himself in total through his love for the princess within himself. His return home would have been a different adventure than the one getting to Deathwall, for he would have let himself experience all the adventures to the fullest.

Of course in the *Dialogs* the illusion was fancied up in visions of female passions, bods for the taking. But in reality they were only illustrations of his own needs, his own passions, his own self.

Well, that's one way to look at the *Dialogs* (as a conflict within Mhyo's own consciousness)! Now he could return to his center and be able to take possession of it all! Only then would he be ready to once more seek Deathwall and move beyond It into the experience of discovering others.

I concluded my statement to Heidi in this way: "You know, one could almost make a claim than the *Dialogs* is a symbolic birthing, the developing of life within the very womb. But, I never thought of it that way. Though I did see the land of walls as being nothing more than the cavity of our own brains, within which we have our consciousness. And the events that took place in the *Dialogs* are but one experience, one inner adventure, just a one Once up on a Timer!

"Now you have seen more of my feelings about the world of walls. And that's why having Roman columns is just fine and dandy. The elements within that land of walls were nothing more than the elements within our personal experience—Mhyo's experience, which certainly contained...."

Well, the above applies only if you believe that the *Dialogs* are fiction and not an ancient doc found in a little shop in India.

—Charles Nuetzel
July 2006

ABOUT THE AUTHOR

Charles Nuetzel was born in San Francisco in 1934, and writes:

"As long as I can remember I wanted to be a writer. It was a dream I never thought would materialize. But with the help of Forrest J Ackerman, who became my agent, I managed to finally make it into print.

"I was lucky enough not only in selling my work to publishers but also ending up packaging books for some of them, and finally becoming a 'publisher' much like those who had bought my first novels. From there it as a simple leap to editing not only a sci-fi anthology, but a line of sci-fi books for Powell Sci-Fi back in the 1960s. Throughout these active professional years I had the chance to design some covers and do graphic cover layouts for pocket books & magazines."

Much of his work in covers and graphics are a result of having had a father who was a professional commercial artist, and who did a number of covers for sci-fi magazines in the 1950s and later for pocket books—even for some of Mr. Nuetzel's books.

In retirement he has become involved in swing dancing, a long time lover of Big Band jazz. But more interestingly world travels have taken him (and his wife Brigitte) across the world, to Hawaii, Caribbean, Mexico, Kenya, Egypt, Peru, having a life-long interest in ancient civilizations. His website is full of thousands of pictures taken during these trips.

www.ingramcontent.com/pod-product-compliance
Lightning Source LLC
Chambersburg PA
CBHW020612250626
47154CB00004B/1474